DEVIL'S SHOESTRING

SPELLS FOR HIRE BOOK ONE

STEFON MEARS

Also by Stefon Mears

Cavan Oltblood Series
Half a Wizard
The Ice Dagger
Spells of Undeath

Spells for Hire
Devil's Shoestring
Zombie Powder
Spirit Trap
Dragon's Blood (coming December 2019)

The Rise of Magic
Magician's Choice
Sleight of Mind
Lunar Alchemy
Three Fae Monte
The Sphinx Principle

The Telepath Trilogy
Surviving Telepathy
Immoral Telepathy
Targeting Telepathy

Edge of Humanity
Caught Between Monsters
Hunting Monsters

Power City Tales
Not Quite Bulletproof
No Money in Heroism

Devil's Night
Portal-Land, Oregon
Stealing from Pirates
Fade to Gold
With a Broken Sword
Twice Against the Dragon
The House on Cedar Street
Sudden Death
On the Edge of Faerie
Confronting Legends (Spells & Swords Vol. 1)
Uncle Stone Teeth and Other Macabre Poems
The Patreon Collection, Vol. 1-4 (Vol. 5, coming soon)

Published by Thousand Faces Publishing, Portland, Oregon

http://1kfaces.com

This book was originally published as *The Patron Saint of Necromancers*.

ISBN: 978-1-948490-12-2

Devil's Shoestring

Spells for Hire | Book One

AUTHOR'S NOTE

Spells for Hire stories take place in a world that is very like our own, but is not our own.

Thus, you might be able to visit some of the locations described in this book, such as the Witch's Castle in Forest Park. Others, however, have been fictionalized or invented whole cloth, like Gripper. Where I have fictionalized or invented, I have tried to maintain that unique Portland vibe.

In much the same way, religions such as Vodou, Candomblé and Shugendō exist in this world, as do other practices such as Hoodoo. I have done substantial research in my attempts to keep my portrayals true to the spirit of those beliefs and practices. I have, however, taken liberties for dramatic purposes. I hope that devotees of those religions and practices will forgive any mistakes I have made.

1

———

Heath stood on the cusp of redemption. Redemption in this case was a bar called Gripper.

From the outside it didn't look like much in the best of times, and in the dying sunlight of a July evening, it looked downright uninviting. No windows in the front. No sign. Nothing to attract the attention of wandering tourists – or worse, locals not in the know who might mistake it for a neighborhood watering hole.

Gripper wasn't looking for people who might be curious about a dog shit brown stucco building sandwiched between a salvage shop and a musical instruments store. People who wanted to talk about the Blazers or the Timbers or the Thorns or the Winterhawks or the Ducks or the Beavers.

The sports fans and the bike-riders and the hipsters could buy their Pabst Blue Ribbon somewhere else. Gripper catered to a specific clientele, and the only people welcome there didn't need a sign to tell them what it was.

Patrons entered through a red door with a purple symbol in the center of the frame that looked like a stylized number four to the casual observer.

Heath knew it was the symbol of Jupiter from one of those musty old grimoires. He still thought it looked like a stylized number four. But planetary magic was Maggie's shtick, and it was her bar.

Not a hundred feet away traffic still buzzed up and down Burnside, some heading across the Willamette for the west side of Portland or points beyond, others on their way back. Everyone in a hurry, but Heath couldn't bring himself to move.

If he was honest with himself, Heath would have admitted nerves did as much to stick his red-and-black Hawaiian shirt to his back as the heat and humidity. But this was not the time for introspection.

This was twilight, that perfect moment when the shadows vanished but the street lights hadn't kicked on. When the whole world grew sharp and clear to the eye. Great time of day to cast certain charms.

And a great time for a drink in the company of his peers.

If he was welcome.

Heath patted the mojo bag in the right pocket of his black jeans, hoisted his backpack a little higher on his right shoulder. He spat left, then right, then knocked. Three knocks, because it was a Thursday.

As the door opened, a hit of air conditioning lifted Heath's spirits immediately, but his breath caught when he saw who was holding the doorknob. She looked like a frail old woman, seventy-five if she was a day under a hundred. Skin so white her wrinkles were all but translucent. Locks of silver gray that dangled to her shoulders and a turquoise dress that fit her like a queenly robe. Powdery-sweet perfume hung about her like a personal fog.

But Mrs. Halloran's green eyes held sharpness that could cut steel. And the silver torc around her neck, twisted Celtic knot work, was the resting place of a familiar spirit with a nasty reputation.

Heath had to swallow hard before he could speak. He could hear laughing and talking and strains of Greek folk music coming from inside, and he drew hope from the merriment. He could even smell a hint of garlic fries past the perfume.

"Good evening, Mrs. Halloran."

She arched an eyebrow as she looked up at him, and allowed just a touch of her old-country Irish lilt to flavor her words when she said, "Heath Cyr. The twilight boy."

Heath forced a tight-lipped smile and ground his teeth. Some people called him "Twilight" because he walked the line between spirits and humans. Others because they considered his magic somewhere between one flavor and another.

Mrs. Halloran turned the occasional nickname into "the twilight boy" because of the color of his skin. Not white as his mother, though his brown curls matched the ones growing out of her scalp. Not black as his father, though their dark brown eyes were a perfect match. Somewhere in between, like so many things in Heath's life.

"Been a long time since you last knocked on this door, Heath Cyr."

"I've been a bit busy."

"Sure, and we've all heard a bit about that. Banished a duke of Hell, some are saying."

Heath chose not to point out that it was a marquis. And that it was less a proper banishment than a remarkable piece of trickery if he said so himself. Instead he gave a noncommittal one-shoulder shrug.

Mrs. Halloran smiled. But she didn't move to let him in. She didn't close the door either, though. Finally, she said, "You weren't thinking I was going to let you in here carrying that bag o' tricks. You haven't been gone that long."

Heath turned a relieved sigh into a chuckle as he handed over his backpack.

Mrs. Halloran moved aside, but before Heath could finish a step she put a hand on his chest.

"Start something tonight, twilight boy, and I'll finish it."

Heath raised his hands in mock surrender. "Never doubted that for a moment. I just want a drink."

Mrs. Halloran looked him up and down, and though she stood a good foot shorter than Heath's six feet, without using the slightest bit of magic she managed to make him feel small.

"I suggest you stick to that."

She moved off then, and Heath let the door close behind him. Air conditioning soothed his skin while he got a good look at the interior of Gripper for the first time in many months. Nothing had changed.

Seven large tables in the center, painted the colors Cornelius Agrippa attributed to the planets in his books. Or at least, that was what Maggie had said when Heath asked why the little square tables were all brown but the big round ones were colorful. Black, blue, red, yellow, green, orange and silver. Like they belonged as marshmallows in a breakfast cereal.

Heath had then asked why not nine? Or at least eight, depending on how she felt about Pluto. That question only got him a smile, but at least Maggie had a good smile.

The ceiling was painted as a star field, black, with swirls of red and blue for nebulae and scores of little lights for the stars. There were floodlights arrayed around the perimeter, if needed, but the little lights kept the bar feeling cozy without getting dim.

Only five patrons so far tonight, all of them people Heath recognized. But his eye was immediately drawn to the bar itself. Not the heavy-set man with the balding pate and the ill-fitting shirt and cargo pants, but the gorgeous Brazilian woman he was talking to.

It wasn't her caramel skin or her soft brown hair or the slender curves barely concealed under the light fabric of her midnight blue dress that drew Heath's attention.

It was the black heart behind the beauty everyone knew as Vizinha.

HEATH SMILED AND FOCUSED ON THE SMELL OF GARLIC FRIES. ANYTHING but the presence of Vizinha, the last person walking this earth he wanted to see right then.

Well, not quite the *last* person, but close enough.

The garlic fries, however, were a Gripper specialty, and the batch smelled fresh. Enticing. Heath hadn't eaten anything since that turkey sandwich around noon. And with Heath's quick metabolism, carbs were a must.

So he inhaled deep the tang of the garlic until he could almost taste the oil of it coat his tongue. And he tried to ignore the flare of adrenaline twitching in his stomach at the sight of Vizinha, so soon after that bout of nerves at the possibility of Gripper turning him away. Tried to pretend his stomach was just growling with hunger.

Vizinha adjusted on her barstool to let him know she'd spotted him, and Heath had to bite his cheek to keep from turning to look at her head-on. Didn't help that the heavy guy she was talking to had blatantly spun around to give Heath an unfriendly gaze.

Heath's hands wanted to pat at his bag of tricks for reassurance, but Mrs. Halloran had it. Yes, there were things he could do without it. Plenty of them. And he even had a trick or two he could have used to get it back, if he were anywhere else. But this was the only bar worth going to for a guy like Heath, and with Vizinha here...

Did Maggie know both he and Vizinha were going to be here tonight? Was that why Mrs. Halloran was watching the door – and right now watching Heath from over near the restrooms to his left?

Wrong direction for his attention.

The smell of the garlic fries wasn't holding his focus, so he listened to the sound of his loafers scuffling on the wooden floor while he made his way between a big orange table and a bigger purple one toward the far end of the bar.

Only felt like the walk took half an hour. That might have been because conversation in the room stopped. The three old witches in the corner – two women and a man, all with enough gray hair to make a quilt – were now watching what Heath did *not* want to turn into a show.

The Greek folk music playing over the hidden speakers came to an end. Now he could hear the boards creak just a little under his weight, and some kind of thumping from back behind the bar.

Still, Heath kept that smile on his face like a shield, while on the inside he prayed, "Papa Legba, keep an eye on this little fool. Make sure nothing bad follows him home tonight."

Finally he reached the bar, and Heath sighed as he eased down onto the padding of the end stool and slid his hands along the bar top. The bar itself had hundreds of star charts lacquered into place along the top and sides. Worn and scuffed now, like Heath felt himself, despite his youth. But the star charts were all intact under the thick coats of lacquer.

Heath tried to take that as a good sign.

No mirror behind the bar. Not at a place like Gripper. The last thing Maggie needed was some idiot getting drunk and calling something up out of a mirror that she would then have to put back down. Instead she had six shelves of alcohols, from the cheapest bourbon anyone could talk themselves into swallowing to a smattering of Irish whiskeys so old that Mrs. Halloran's grandmother might have been on a first-name basis with them.

And that didn't count the unofficial things that Maggie didn't keep on display, but everyone knew she had. Old school absinthe replete with wormwood, tequila flavored with spirit worms, ouzo with a touch of hemlock, and others Heath could barely remember.

The tension in the room began to weigh on him. It seemed that everyone expected him to say something. He started drumming his fingers as though he felt relaxed, instead of tight enough to snap in a strong breeze. He could feel Vizinha's eyes on him.

Maggie bustled in from the back of the bar carrying a cardboard box. Heath always thought Maggie looked like an ex-boxer, complete with the broken nose and the muscled kind of fitness under her black tee shirt and blue jeans that some guys found sexy. She kept her red hair buzzed close, completing the image. Her one concession to the traditional American ideas of femininity was the touch of eye makeup she wore to highlight her clear blue irises.

The moment Maggie saw Heath she stopped and smiled. And just like that the tension shifted. Maggie's smile had that kind of effect on rooms.

Vizinha went back to talking to her companion. Heath could

place the guy now. Drake, short for Mandrake. The kind of guy who liked to put on robes, fire up the incense, and conjure demons in his living room. The kind who called himself a Karcist.

"Heard you did a big favor for one of the homeless-by-choice kids," Maggie said, setting down the box on the floor where no one else could see what was in it. Maggie called everyone younger than her a kid, even though she couldn't have been more than five years older than Heath, which would have made her about thirty.

Not that Heath would ask.

Maggie grabbed a pilsner glass and started filling it with Deschutes Hefeweizen. "Convinced a demon not to kill him because he was already dead or something?"

"Something like that. Wasn't a favor though, unless you count undercharging him."

"*Under*charging?" said Vizinha. "For *your* work? Is that possible?"

Heath started to turn, but caught himself. Instead he took the beer when Maggie offered it.

"Well, you impressed the hell out of the kid anyway," said Maggie loudly, "and *we've all heard.*"

"Yeah," said Heath with a chuckle. "Got the feeling he was going to use that story to get people buying him drinks all over town." He raised his glass to Maggie. "Very good for business."

Heath savored the crisp taste of the Hef while Maggie turned her attention to putting things away under the bar.

"You shouldn't have interfered."

Harsh words, but a man with a high voice has to work to sound impressive. Heath turned to see the speaker, Drake, glaring at him. Vizinha smiled and fluttered her chestnut eyes at Heath.

"A client came to me with a problem," said Heath with a shrug. "Don't see how that's any of your business."

"Depends on who sent that demon," said Vizinha. "Doesn't it?"

Heath spun his stool so he faced them both.

"Is that what this is about?" he said to Vizinha, talking right past Drake. "Kicking my ass last year wasn't good enough for you?"

"There will be no fighting in here," said Maggie, not pausing whatever she was doing under the bar. "So keep it civil."

"Look," said Heath to Drake. "I don't know what your issue was with the guy, and I don't care. You want to go after him again, go for it. But if he comes back to me for help, well, I've got to pay my bar tab somehow, don't I?"

"Too right," said Maggie, still clinking bottles down there like she was either looking for something or getting to her spring cleaning very late.

"You need a lesson," said Drake, standing up. He threw a twenty down on the bar. He narrowed his eyes at Heath and nodded slowly. "Yes, you do."

Exit Drake, stage right, pursuing Furies.

Heath sighed and sipped at his beer, but Vizinha was still staring at him. Smiling.

"What?" he finally said, without looking.

"Oh, nothing," she said. "I wouldn't want to raise a dead issue."

She pulled a fifty from her cleavage and dropped it on the bar before sauntering out like she was walking a runway.

"Maggie?" said Heath. When she popped her head up to look at him, he continued, "Do other people get to drink here without getting threatened?"

"All the time," she said. But then she winked. "But not the interesting ones."

***

HEATH STAYED ANOTHER COUPLE OF HOURS AT GRIPPER, AND BY THE time he left he'd remembered why he liked the place. It was in full swing – two dozen patrons scattered around, talking loudly over the Irish folk music now coming out of those hidden speakers. A young couple in the corner even danced.

And without Vizinha staring him down, Heath enjoyed himself. Three games of darts. A good conversation about High John the

Conqueror root with a pair of *curanderos* who worked around the east Portland suburbs of Gresham and Milwaukee. Even two small commissions – cowrie shell readings for competent practitioners who trusted their magic for everything but divination.

Nothing like leaving a bar with more money in his pocket than when he came in. Heath was all but whistling when Mrs. Halloran handed him his backpack beside the front door.

"Practically a welcome back party for you," she said, holding onto one strap to keep him from taking the backpack just yet.

"Oh, they were testing me all night. Details about the big story. Wanting to know what work I'd been doing lately." Heath shrugged. "Making sure Vizinha didn't shatter my nerve."

More than fifteen forms of magic practiced by the people in this bar tonight, from shamans to western ceremonialists to Druids to Taoist sorcerers. And every one of those systems agreed on a single truth – magic was for those who dared.

"A fair question." Those sharp eyes were probing for something. "You were gone a long time."

Why wouldn't she let go of the backpack?

Heath looked at her hand, then back at her.

"Is there something you want to know?"

"Everyone knows she took you down. Brigid knows you never denied it. But no one seems to know *why*."

Heath felt his joy at the evening ebb away.

"And no one needs to," he said in a hard voice. "Now if you don't mind, I'd like to leave."

"All right, all right," she said, a mocking smile edging her lips as she let go of the backpack. "It's my duty as door guardian to remind you that you've been threatened twice tonight. Once explicitly by Mandrake. Once implicitly by Vizinha. As soon as you pass though this door, I am no longer responsible for you. So try not to get killed."

That last made Heath blink, but she must have seen his quizzical expression because before he could ask she added, "I'm not eager to see my granddaughter cry, and I think she'd miss you."

"Good night, Mrs. Halloran."

The old bat said something noncommittal as she moved off, and Heath opened the door, though he took a moment to gather himself before stepping across the threshold. He should have thought to prepare for this in advance. Instead, he couldn't leave without improvising. And it had to be something quick and easy, or he'd draw the attention of the whole bar again.

He dug through his backpack past the candles and bags of herbs and other paraphernalia for his pure silver, ten-ounce flask. He uncapped it and waved it back and forth in front of himself, where the cinnamon flavoring of the thrice-blessed rum could tempt his own nose as well as the spirits.

"Papa Legba, tap your cane. Distract my enemies so they don't see me as I pass." He poured some rum on the sidewalk. "Papa Legba, tap your cane. Confuse my enemies so they can't hear my footsteps as I pass." More rum. "Papa Legba, tap your cane. Help me get home swift and safe."

One last jigger of rum on the sidewalk, then Heath capped the flask and started walking toward the Max station with a confident stride. He slipped the flask into his bag, and just on the edge of his hearing he began to detect a distant tapping sound.

The lights were green for Heath, and he reached the Max station and boarded his light rail train just as the doors were closing so it could depart. All the bench seats of the car around him were empty, but the air felt foggy. Misty almost. And syncopated with the bumps and jolts of the rolling train heading west, he could hear a distant tapping as of wood on concrete.

That tapping continued as he left the train and walked through a sleepy northwest neighborhood to his apartment near tremendous Forest Park.

Once upon a time, Heath's apartment had been a guest house, or perhaps an in-law house, in the backyard of a good-sized home. But that family was gone now, and whoever bought the land had gotten the permits to turn the house itself into four apartments. And the management company, well, they seemed to have gone and forgotten about that little guest house.

Oh, Heath was sure they hadn't forgotten it entirely. But they hadn't raised his rent in six years, and he didn't pay any of his own utilities. Not even cable, Internet or telephone. In fact, Heath suspected he could have stopped paying rent and G&H Management might never have noticed.

But that would have been wrong. And Heath had no intention of offending whatever spirits were keeping him in a spacious, stand-alone one-bedroom apartment with its own loft and basement for five hundred fifty dollars a month. So every month he paid his rent, and when he did he set out an extra offering to those unnamed spirits.

Wouldn't do to be ungrateful.

Monthly gardeners kept the local native plants in line in that backyard. Ferns, roses, rhododendrons, Oregon grapes, and of course tall, mighty Douglas fir trees. A half-dozen of them. Heath's apartment was practically situated in the woods. He even liked to sit on his little front porch on a nice spring evening when he did his carving.

Unlike the bar, Heath's front door was white, with a hand-painted, black, equal-armed cross and old fashioned key. Not as formal as the veves of Vodou, but it served as his own connection to Papa Legba at the threshold.

Heath heard the tapping all the way to that front door, and it didn't stop until that door was closed and locked behind him.

"Thank you, Papa," Heath whispered, leaning back against that door in the darkness.

Someone knocked.

THE SHARP SOUND MADE HEATH JUMP, BUT HE DROPPED HIS BACKPACK by choice. He kept the lights off, and reached down beside the doorframe for his tire thumper. Eighteen inches of aluminum bat.

"Who's there?" he said through the closed door, smelling the

Hefeweizen on his own breath. Surely no one could have followed him. Not with Papa Legba tapping his cane.

"Could you open the door, please, Mr. Cyr?" Man's voice. Someone used to authority. Didn't identify as police, though, which Heath considered a good thing. He'd never had uncalled-for police show up at his door for a good reason.

"It's closing in on eleven o'clock at night, and I'm not expecting any visitors. That means you're trespassing. So I'd appreciate it if you left without my calling the cops."

"You'll have a hard time proving trespassing, Mr. Cyr. Since I own the land."

Heath shook his head and turned on the porch light. He opened the door, not trying to hide the tire thumper in his grip. The man standing there was wasn't too much older than Heath. He had a thick, Scottish jaw and nose, and hair black enough to vanish against a midnight sky. He had the kind of white skin that had red undertones.

And he was wearing a black suit, with an unwrinkled white shirt and a black tie.

Who wore suits at this time of night?

With the door open, Heath could hear the frogs and crickets discussing this strange man on his porch. They didn't sound like they liked his presence any better than Heath did.

"I suppose you have a deed or some other kind of proof of that, do you?" said Heath.

"I do." The man patted the left side of his chest, implying paperwork in a jacket pocket. "But rather than dig it out, let me prove it this way. Six months ago I was auditing the work of my management company and noticed that more money was coming in from this location than expected. Would you care to guess how much?"

Heath got a sinking feeling in his stomach. Six months ago would have been at about the height of the problems Vizinha had sent his way during their war.

"Well, I did a little digging and found an old rental contract that everyone else seems to have forgotten about. Looks like you've been enjoying quite the bargain, wouldn't you say?"

"If you're here to evict me—"

"Perish the thought." The suited man said the words just the way Heath's daddy used to say them, which made Heath wonder if the suited man had lived in New Orleans. "I've done some checking around about you. You seem to be a model tenant, for what that's worth. Never any noise complaints, no calls to the police. Your checks have arrived on the third day of the month like clockwork, and if you've ever needed a plumber or anything, I can't find a record of it."

"So you just wanted to meet me?" Heath smiled, but deep down he knew he couldn't get rid of the suited man this easily. "Well, I'm glad to make your acquaintance. Now if you'll excuse me—"

"But that wasn't all I found out." The man tilted his head to the side. "Rumor has it that you make your money selling Voodoo charms."

"No, that's not right." Heath shook his head with the certainty of absolute truth.

"But I heard about a conjure hand you put together for a man named Jenkins—"

"Hang on." Heath narrowed his eyes at the suited man and got a smile for his troubles. "Most of my clients don't even know the term 'conjure hand.' Not in this part of the country. They all call them mojo bags, and so does Jenkins. What do you know about it?"

"The question, Mr. Cyr, is what do *you* know?"

Heath stared at the man and sighed. He stepped out on the front porch and locked the door behind him, tire thumper still in one hand. Just in case. In the background the frogs and crickets got worked up over this development.

"Why did you try to snow me with Vodou talk? Obviously you know I'm a conjure man."

"I haven't lived in New Orleans since I was a kid," the suited man said. "I can't keep all the terms straight."

"Well," and Heath realized he was raising the tire thumper in what might have been interpreted as a threatening manner, but he didn't lower it. "Hoodoo is magic and Vodou is religion. Seems pretty clear to me."

The suited man stared at the glistening aluminum of the tire thumper.

"I hope I haven't given offense."

"Not to me." Heath shrugged and lowered the tire thumper. "But if you go telling people I claim to practice Vodou, you'll likely offend *them* on my behalf. Then you and I will have a problem."

"All right," the suited man said, raising his hands in surrender, then straightening his tie. "Mind if I get to the point then?"

"I'd like nothing better."

"Mind if we go inside? This is a private matter."

"Nope." Heath shook his head. "I don't discuss business in the house."

The suited man grimaced and looked about, and Heath began to think he'd get the rest of the evening to himself after all, but the suited man finally nodded.

"All right then. Here it is. I presume you know who Saint Cyprian is?"

"Which one?" Heath stifled a yawn. He was just about talked out for the night.

"You know which one. Revered by practitioners of the *ars magica*. They call him the patron saint of—"

"Necromancers. Sure. Cyprian of Antioch." Maybe Heath could find a way to speed this along. "Not that the Church would agree with the common folk about that patronage. What about him?"

"Do *you* revere him?" The suited man got intense with that question, holding his breath and staring at Heath as though he could see through to Heath's soul.

"Can't say I've had much to do with him. I use Saint Cyprian oil when it's called for – and I make my own oils – but that's about it. I'm not one of those guys who keeps a statue of him and goes through the whole annual nine-day ritual to him or anything, if that's what you're asking."

The suited man continued staring for a moment, tempting Heath to raise the tire thumper again. But finally the suited man nodded.

"I believe you."

"Well thank God for that," said Heath. "It was going to keep me up all night. Can I—"

"And I want to hire you. The true *Black Book of Saint Cyprian* has been found, and I want you to get it for me."

The frogs and crickets stopped chattering.

2

____

HEATH STARED AT THE STRANGE, SUITED MAN BY THE YELLOW LIGHT OF his front porch. In Granddad's stories, the devil was always a white man with black hair, wearing a black suit. Just like this man in front of him.

That couldn't be a coincidence. And Heath would have sworn there was a chill in the air that he didn't usually feel on a nice July evening.

The garlic fries and beer shifted uncomfortably in his belly.

"You've got the wrong man," Heath said at last. "Having problems with your woman? Or man, I don't judge. I can help you out. I can help you find one too, if you're lonely." Heath leaned his tire thumper against his shoulder. "You need some protection, or a little luck, or the solution to any one of those problems that make life unbearable, I can do the job for you for a fair price."

He shook his head. "But I'm not some kind of treasure hunter and I'm not a detective. And I'm not going to go running around like your errand boy. You want a book, I suggest you go to Powell's. It's right down Burnside. You can't miss it."

"Mr. Cyr, I realize that this sounds ... unusual—"

"No," Heath said slowly. "Unusual is what puts food on my table.

What this is, is a waste of my time. I can name you three translations of Saint Cyprian's grimoire off the top of my head. And I can pretty much guarantee Powell's will have at least two of—"

"Forgeries!" The suited man paused to straighten his tie again, and seemed to recover himself in the process. "The Catholic Church has allowed those forgeries to circulate because they contain just enough magic to convince hopefuls of their veracity, and too little to be useful. Or to make anyone look outside the Church for miracles."

"What," said Heath, listening with half an ear for the frogs and crickets to pick up their conversation, "you're going to tell me the true grimoire was hidden in some secret Vatican vault?"

The suited man raised his eyebrows in the clearest "duh" expression Heath had seen this side of the downtown hipsters.

"Why do you think Pope Benedict left office so soon?" the suited man asked. "He screwed up. *The Black Book* was stolen on his watch, which proved him fallible even when acting on behalf—"

"You're saying he was kicked out? Because *this book* was stolen from secret Vatican vaults?"

The suited man nodded, once.

"Have you tried telling Dan Brown?"

"Mr. Cyr, I—"

"Look, Suit, you want a spell to bring you this book? Fine. I'll charge you a special landlord rate and give you my best effort. But if it's as in-demand as it sounds like, I'm not going to guarantee results. Too many others will be throwing spells after this like it's—"

"No."

Suit looked Heath up and down, and in that moment Heath cursed inwardly. He'd let this stranger get to him. Given him a nickname.

Giving personal nicknames was a practice Heath usually reserved for clients. Every client got a nickname, that way it never mattered if he learned their name or not. He had a designation that would prove more than accurate enough if he had to send something to a client's window at night for non-payment.

The only non-clients who got nicknames were strangers who

pissed Heath off enough that he was seriously considering hexing them.

But hexing his landlord was not Heath's idea of a good way to promote a long and healthy landlord-tenant relationship.

"Mr. Cyr, I have not come to you for a spell. As you say, right now there must be hundreds of people trying to draw the *Black Book* to them by magic. And when that many attempt it, the chances of any of them succeeding—"

"Fall away to zero." Heath stretched his face in thought as he looked closer at Suit. Memories of Granddad's stories flitted around the back of his mind. "So you know a thing or two, do you? Don't feel like you have much juju to you though."

"I have not yet rung the astral bell."

Heath snorted. Of all the ridiculous, highfalutin expressions...

"Look," said Heath. "I'm going to tell you something I'd tell anyone in your position. Something I wish I'd been able to stop and think about with a clear head when the time came for me."

Heath leaned a little closer, free hand open in a soothing gesture and tire thumper held down and away so it didn't threaten.

"Walk away. Just turn your back on all this magic stuff and go live a safe life. You're obviously a rich man, so buy yourself a hobby. A yacht, a sports team, whatever the hell you rich people do. Buy a spell or a conjure hand if you want to feel a thrill and dance on the edge while you make changes in your life."

Heath let out a slow breath, wondering if he was getting through to Suit at all. Suit's face looked just as blank as the ocean – he could tell something was going on under the surface, but he had no idea what.

"But don't set your first step down this path. Because once you start, you don't get to stop. And you're going to find out there's a whole lot more to this world than you ever wanted to know."

"I appreciate the warning, but you will not dissuade a man who prizes knowledge with the argument that there are things man was not meant to know."

"Meant to know, hell. I'm talking about things you *don't want* to know. I sure don't want to know them."

And just like that, Suit closed up. Heath hadn't thought he'd seen much expression on that ruddy-pale face, but it smoothed completely as Suit straightened and adjusted his tie again. Like someone had flicked his switch.

"Mr. Cyr, I appreciate that you regret choices you have made in life, but those regrets are immaterial to this conversation."

"Fine," said Heath with a shrug. "I'd say this conversation is over anyway. I've got some roots I want to grind before midnight—"

"We are not done yet."

Heath raised his eyebrows and settled his tire thumper casually against his shoulder.

"You were worried about eviction, but I think you know I have no legal reason to seek that. However, I am well within my legal rights to raise your rent. But that's not all. Were you aware that utilities are not mentioned anywhere in your rental agreement? I can have them turned off immediately, and they would not be turned on again until you manage to set up your own accounts and get technicians out here to handle activation. Could take days. Maybe weeks. Hate to see you go that long without water, heat, electricity..."

Suit had the gall to blink innocently. "Also, I spoke with my lawyer this afternoon. I might be able to pursue a claim against you for back utilities, given that I never had any legal obligation to provide them. Also—"

"Pretty sure I get your point." Heath smiled his old retail cashier smile, the one with a strong fuck-you undertone. "And you could do all that. Of course, karma's a bitch. The universe might smack you down for this sort of thing. You know. Ruin your businesses, make you impotent, hit you with one nasty disease or another. All sorts of troubles raining down on your head."

"That sounds like a threat."

"Does it?" Heath scratched his chin. "Here I just thought I was telling you how the universe doesn't like nasty people. I mean, if I wanted to threaten you I'm already holding a bat. And besides, legally speaking, there's no such thing as magic, right?"

"My point is, matters need not come to this. I am prepared to offer you a deal that I think will serve us both much better."

"A deal where I have to dig you up a book I don't believe exists?"

"I have proof that it does. And this is a deal where you get a written guarantee that this is your home as long as you want to live here, rent free, utilities on me, complete with any upgrades needed to keep it current."

An urge to whistle appreciatively tried to work its way up Heath's throat. That could come to hundreds of thousands of tax-free dollars over the course of a few decades. But Heath clamped down that urge before it reached the back of his mouth, much less his lips.

"Not much of a guarantee if you sell the land, even to a shell company you own."

Suit smiled and gave a gracious nod.

"The guarantee will include language that prevents the land from being sold unless the buyer agrees in a separate contract to maintain all the same terms for you. Someone else buys it, you still get the same deal. Even if it's flipped again."

"Starting to sound reasonable," said Heath, shaking his head. "Still—"

"There would, of course, be a fee for your troubles — say, twenty-three thousand, six hundred sixty seven dollars — plus reimbursement for reasonable expenses." Suit extended his hand, with a broad smile that made Heath itch along his spine. "Do we have a deal?"

Heath had to hand it to Suit. It was a fair price, and the man knew how to offer payment to a conjure man. Root magic doesn't deal in round numbers.

"First I have to know something," said Heath. "Why me?"

"Because I don't think you'll want to keep the book for yourself." Suit lowered his hand and shrugged, such a slight movement of his shoulders that he might have been adjusting the fit of his jacket. "I can't say that about the others I've considered for this."

The frogs and crickets started up again. They didn't believe Suit was telling the whole truth, and neither did Heath.

But he couldn't deny that the offer was reasonable. And he loved his apartment too much to just walk away from it.

"All right, then."

Suit offered his hand again to shake.

Heath looked at it. Shook his head. "When I see the paperwork. *Then* we have a deal, and then I will get to work. In the meantime, I have a thousand..."

Heath's words trailed off as Suit's lips stretched in a smile. Suit reached into the pocket of his jacket. He pulled out a contract, and as Heath looked over the terms he felt a fresh wash of cold down his face and spine.

Every point they'd discussed was covered. Just as though Suit knew exactly what deal he was going to get. And maybe that was all it was. Maybe Suit was just a good negotiator.

But as Heath signed on the dotted line, he couldn't help thinking about Granddad and his stories.

THE NEXT MORNING SAW STORM CLOUDS MOVING IN FROM THE WEST, but Heath didn't pay them any attention. If this were January, or even May, those clouds might have settled overhead for a good long rain. But this was July, one of the two or three months Portland could count on for actual sunlight.

Those clouds didn't have a chance. They'd be burnt away by noon at the latest.

So Heath threw on another pair of black jeans and a light, blue-and-white striped shirt with short sleeves, a collar, and a pocket where he could tuck a couple of little extras in case he needed them. Then he hoisted his backpack and headed off for a breakfast meeting with two of the only human allies he knew he could count on.

The meeting was at Tsarina's, a marvelous little hole-in-the-wall Russian place on Front Avenue, hidden away in the industrial section of northwest, near the Willamette. Everywhere around Tsarina's were parking lots full of semis and buses, all fenced in behind alarms and razor wire, and warehouses in ice cream colors with long, rounded tops like tiny, repurposed airplane hangars. Fewer trees per square foot than any other part of Portland, which made it only ten times greener than the section of Manhattan where Heath grew up.

Tsarina's was long as a rail car, and so narrow it only accommodated five army surplus folding tables along one wall – three folding chairs each – leaving a single path from the front door to the counter. The tables all had cheap, red-and-white checkered tablecloths, and narrow glass vases that each held an orange Gerber daisy. The floor echoed like hollow aluminum no matter who was walking across it, and along the walls were old photographs of the last Russian royal family. Actual photos, not printouts or newspaper cut-outs, and small enough to have been family mementos.

Tsarina's was the kind of place that only had one employee bathroom back behind the counter. If you were a customer, you got to use it if they liked you. If they didn't, it was out of order.

They probably lost customers that way, but as far as Heath could tell, they didn't care. The two tables nearest the counter were always full of old men speaking Russian, and though Heath didn't come here as often as he liked, he would have sworn they were always the same men.

Fans blew hard from back in the kitchen, carrying rich, meaty smells at any time of day, and easing the summer heat.

Colin was already waiting, sitting with his back to the door at the first table, when Heath let the aluminum screen door slam shut behind him.

Colin had that skinny, long-haired white kid look that Heath thought of as stoner chic. Fine blonde hair. Skin so pale it might burn under artificial light. Old blue jeans, faded and paint-stained in some places and worn in others, and certainly in no better shape than his sneakers. An Iron Maiden tee shirt from a tour that must have been before Colin was born. He was in his third year at the University of

Portland, studying guitar, and practiced the oddest magic Heath had ever run across.

Despite appearances, Colin never smelled like pot, not even since recreational use became legal in Oregon. He smelled like baked goods. Today it was cinnamon rolls.

"Did you eat *before* a breakfast meeting?" asked Heath as he took the seat facing Colin.

"Haven't been to bed yet. I was really feeling the transcription of this Vivaldi piece and it wouldn't let me rest, you know?"

"*Four Seasons*?"

"Pffft. So last year. *Cello Sonata No.4 in B flat major, RV45.*"

Heath stared blankly. Colin snickered like a cartoon dog.

"Cretin."

"I prefer my music to have complicated drum rhythms."

Before Colin could voice his rejoinder, the aluminum door slammed to announce the entrance of Nariko.

Almost as tall as Heath, Nariko had the misfortune of growing up with the kind of willowy beauty that attracted American Japanophiles by the truckload. Her twin sister Michiko dealt with this problem by cutting her glittering black hair short and wearing frumpy pants and tops to downplay what good genes had given her. She went so far as to hide her jade eyes behind hideous frames even though she didn't need glasses.

Nariko took the opposite approach. She wore skirts and flimsy tops with her long hair down when she was casual, and tight jeans and form-fitting shirts with a tight bun when she was working, like today. As for the hopefuls, she cut down on their approaches with a resting bitch face that could shatter concrete.

She took the wall-facing chair, spun it around, and plopped down with her arms folded across the back.

"What's shakin', bitches?"

"Heath has no appreciation for classical music."

"You should see him when he hears bagpipes. Like a cat heading for the ceiling."

"That was *one time...*" Heath stopped as soon as he saw them both grin. "Look. Can we discuss my musical tastes later?"

"Just as soon as you develop some," said Colin.

Heath was saved from replying because Inga cleared her throat. Heath didn't know if Inga owned Tsarina's or just ran it, but it wasn't the sort of place that encouraged questions.

Either way, Inga was built like a five-and-a-half-foot tall potato, right down to a blotchy complexion. The dark brown dresses she wore only encouraged the image in Heath's mind. She had lots of yellow-blond hair and bound it into tight braids that she wound round and round the top of her head. But she smiled her slightly scary smile at the customers she liked, and she was smiling then when she said, "Heath, I know, will have his two breakfast *pirozhkis* with coffee watered to down to American levels. And you two?"

"I'll have a breakfast *pirozhki*," said Nariko, pronouncing it better than Heath would have, "but I'll take my coffee at the same strength you'd drink it, Inga."

Inga nodded with approval, then had to pull out a pad of paper to write down Colin's order, which would have been enough to feed a family of six that hadn't eaten in a week. She took the whole order with one eyebrow raised, but said nothing until he finished.

"This is all?"

"For now." Colin smiled, teeth white enough for a dental poster.

When Inga left the table, Heath told them what he was after and why.

Nariko shook her head, one eyebrow raised in her "fool" expression, while Colin whistled.

"I have a couple of good spirits for finding books," said Colin, "but something like that..."

"You undercharged," said Nariko. "As always."

"If I live there another forty years—"

"If you survive getting your hands on the book in the first place." Nariko stroked Heath's cheek, the tender way she used to, lips quirking in a half-smile when she said, "You're sweet, but you're dumb in all the wrong ways."

Colin snickered, and Heath felt heat creep up his neck.

"I was talking about *business*," Nariko said archly.

"I signed the contract," said Heath, "so until I know that this is a lot more involved than he told me I need to do my due diligence and find out what I'm in for. Will you guys help me?"

"I don't know, man," said Colin. "I could maybe find out something about your biggest competitors, but this kind of thing isn't as hands-off as I like to work."

"I suppose I better," said Nariko. "You're too pretty to be a corpse. But you owe me for this one. Big time."

"You know I'm good for it."

Whatever Nariko would have said next was lost when a big block of a man kicked the door open. He smelled like olives, wore a trench coat despite the heat, and looked as though every bone in his face had been broken and set wrong. His coat had a spell or two on it. Something to do with disguise, and something else for protection. Trench Coat leveled a submachine gun at the room.

"I'm looking for Heath Cyr," he rumbled.

"This is why I eat before our breakfast meetings," said Colin.

<hr>

Trench Coat's black eyes were just coming to rest on Heath when Inga stormed out of her kitchen. Her heavy steps reverberated through Tsarina's aluminum floor like an earthquake. Her frame filled the aisle between the tables and the wall.

At the two tables nearest the counter, the old Russian men stopped talking.

"You missed him," said Inga. "Heath Cyr has come and gone and now you scare my customers? *My* customers? Waving a popgun around *Tsarina's*? Little boy, you are playing in the street. Toddle along home before someone runs you over."

Trench Coat blinked in a moment of shocked confusion, the barrel of his submachine gun edging toward the ceiling before lowering again toward Inga.

Heath seized the moment to snatch a tiny wax paper envelope from his shirt pocket. He blew orange dust into Trench Coat's face. Trench Coat's eyes fluttered and he passed out on the spot.

"I'm out of here," said Colin. "Inga, I'm sorry I—"

"Go, all of you," she said. "Leave this one to me. He must learn not to do such things here."

Colin was out the door before Inga finished talking.

"I—" started Heath, but Inga interrupted him.

"I will send your food to your home. Your meals are on Tsarina's. This should never have happened here."

"But he was here for..."

Heath's words died when he saw the look on Inga's face. She had the dead eyes of a woman who had killed before. Perhaps often. Perhaps even enjoyed it. Nariko grabbed Heath's hand and led him out the front door, stepping over Trench Coat as they went.

"Let me guess," said Nariko, her eyes scanning the streets. Normal daytime traffic, which here on Front Avenue meant only two or three moving cars in sight. "You didn't drive."

"No," said Heath, watching the areas opposite wherever she looked, but nothing immediately caught his eye. "Never when I don't have to."

He could hear shouts and loud bangs and the rumbles of giant engines in the background, and he was sure he could smell diesel on the building breeze. But these were just the sounds and smells of the local workers. He spotted Trench Coat's car, a rented pick-up truck with the motor running and the driver's door open. No one in it.

"Bitch seat for you then, unless you want to risk his truck."

"I think Tsarina's might be a front for the Russian mob."

"Dumb in all the wrong ways," said Nariko, half-dragging Heath to her sleek, silver motorcycle. A BMW, but Heath didn't know the details, only that it was big. And enchanted. Nariko practiced an Eastern flavor of magic called Shugendō that Heath didn't quite understand. Somewhere between Taoism and Shintoism, and the way she'd once explained her bike to Heath, a combination of harmony and her ancestors kept her safe from tickets and accidents.

The ancestor part Heath got. But he had no idea how harmony entered into the equation.

"Hang on," she said, saddling up and kick-starting the bike. She raised an eyebrow. "But not *too* tight."

"One sec." Heath trotted over to Trench Coat's truck, Nariko rolling her bike after him. He slipped a piece of chalk out of his shirt pocket and drew three crosses on the hood, then uttered the final line of a Unitarian service for the dead.

The truck died with a sputter.

Heath swung onto the bike behind Nariko, and tried not to think about how good it felt to have his arms around her again.

She kicked the bike into gear, and in moments they were speeding along the streets of Portland. The wind whipping through his hair brought back memories of trips together down the coast. Times when her hair was down and buffeting his face.

But today the wind smelled like rain, which was ridiculous. And the storm clouds were still rolling in up above, dark and threatening. And showing no sign of burning off.

Nariko took a left when she should have taken a right, as though she wanted to get on I5 south or head downtown.

"Forgotten the way to my place?" he asked at a stoplight.

"Four cars back. The sedan."

Heath tilted his head around until he could get the right angle in the bike's left side mirror to see a white sedan tucked in between two big SUVs. Two men inside, with deep tans, short black hair, and trench coats.

"Pull over," said Heath.

"Like Hell," said Nariko, emphasizing her point by slipping between cars to cut to the front of the line.

"We can't get away from them."

"Watch me." Nariko revved the engine like she was thinking of jumping the light.

"I didn't get to Tsarina's by car, but they followed me by car? Doesn't make sense. They've got a tracker on me. Might as well talk to them now."

Nariko narrowed her eyes at Heath.

"Who sends a submachine gun when they want to talk?"

"Got rid of Colin. Got us out of Tsarina's. Put us on the run. The only way we reclaim the initiative…"

Nariko snorted and jerked her head back around, revving the engine.

The light changed.

She eased her bike around the corner and rolled it to a stop in a Dairy Queen parking lot. Both she and Heath made a point of watching the white sedan ease on past.

"So much for talking," said Nariko.

"Give them a second."

No more than a minute later, the white sedan returned and pulled into the driveway, parking in a spot near Heath and Nariko, but not too near. The two beefy men got out of their car, hands held out to show that they were empty.

Heath smirked at Nariko.

"Maybe I'm not so dumb after all," he said.

"Jury's still out on that one."

Four other cars in the Dairy Queen parking lot, but the people they belonged to were all inside the restaurant. As places to hold a public conversation went, this one wasn't bad. The MAX line went right past, light rail trains going back and forth to Beaverton and parts beyond. Office buildings across the street, and an exotic furniture store taking up most of the block past the Dairy Queen, complete with its own underground garage.

Traffic. People. Bystanders. Maybe even witnesses, if things went wrong. Heath slung his backpack around and slipped one hand inside it. Not grabbing anything just yet, but ready all the same.

The big beefy guys approached slowly, their eyes flicking to the backpack then back to Heath and Nariko. Like the would-be assailant with the submachine gun, they smelled like olives.

"That's close enough," said Nariko, when they were still a dozen steps away.

They stopped.

"You can see our hands," said the one on the left. He had a horizontal scar under his right eye, maybe two inches long and puckered. "How about returning the favor?"

"Can't say I'm feeling too inclined that direction," said Heath. "Not after your friend with the submachine gun."

"Don't know what you're talking about," said Scar. His partner, who had a heavier, wider jaw, shook his head.

"Of course you don't," said Heath. "What do you guys want?"

"My name is Marvin," said the one with the scar, and Heath decided that would do as well as anything else. "And my friend here is Jarvis."

"Marvin and Jarvis?" said Nariko. "Look, I get not admitting to knowing a guy who would waltz into a restaurant carrying a weapon that might be illegal even here in the PNW, where the firearms roam wild and free. But if you're just going to bullshit us—"

"I'll prove it."

Jarvis looked dubious, but Marvin nodded. Each man slowly opened wide his trench coat and eased a hand inside an interior pocket to pull out a wallet. They retrieved driver's licenses and tossed them on the ground at Nariko's feet.

She picked them up while Heath kept an eye Marvin and Jarvis. "Marvin Spillane and Jarvis Bonetti. Pretty good fakes."

"They're real," said Marvin. "And those are our birth dates and addresses. All real. I'm telling you that because I want to make sure you know that we know what it means to give you that information, Mr. Cyr."

Nariko held up the I.D.s and Heath glanced at them. He nodded. "I'm listening."

"Now, we were told to take you out. I advised against it. As you can see, Jarvis and I live across the river in Vancouver. We've heard a few things about you. And what we've heard suggested that hitting you might not be the smartest approach here."

"Ask your partner how it went," said Nariko, still holding onto the driver's licenses.

"I don't have to. Mr. Cyr, my employers know who you are, and they know that you've been hired to retrieve a certain book. They have an interest in this book as well, and wish to remove you from the equation."

"Don't see how you think threats are a better option than guns," said Heath.

Something was off about these two. Something Heath couldn't quite put his finger on. Spells on their trench coats, just like Mr. Submachine Gun.

But why would they be disguised if they were offering up their identities? Something didn't add up.

"You misunderstand me," said Marvin. "I'm not offering you violence, I'm offering you money. Money has little meaning for my employers, and we can arrange a great deal of it to—"

"Drop your trench coats," said Heath.

"I beg your pardon?"

"Drop them on the ground and step away from them. If you're honest about who you are—"

"Duck!" Nariko grabbed Heath and yanked them both to the asphalt. Something whistled through the air where they'd been standing.

"Damn it," said Heath, pulling out a handful of salt with a few things mixed in. He flung it at Marvin and Jarvis while spitting out the phrase, "Through Your Grace my eyes are open."

Something relaxed inside Heath that he hadn't known was tense. Nothing changed about the appearance of Marvin and Jarvis, except that they seemed less important. They no longer captured Heath and Nariko's attention as they had a moment before.

And now Heath could see a small, blurry red shape swirling through the air. Not much bigger than a stellar jay.

Marvin and Jarvis ran for their car.

Nariko rolled away from Heath, trying to force the red blur to split its attention.

The red blur careened toward Heath. He dove and rolled, one hand frantically digging in his backpack. "I.D.!" he screamed at Nariko.

The blur whistled past again, opening a cut on Heath's cheek. He could hear Marvin and Jarvis start their car. They tried to peel out, but their sedan wasn't quite up to the task. Though Heath could hear it give its all as his hand grasped what he needed.

Nariko tossed the cards at Heath like shuriken, one spinning well wide but the other landing at his feet.

The red blur spun down again. Heath slammed his body to the asphalt of the parking lot. Something bit a tiny chunk out of his neck as the blur flew past. A cold feeling spread out from the spot where the thing bit him.

Heath smeared blood from his cheek on the I.D. It was Marvin's. Next he spat on it. Finally he anointed it with oil ground together from adder's tongue, master root and devil's pod.

"Take the blood. Take the spit. And take your curse you son of a bitch!"

Heath flung the driver's license at the blur as it dove for another attack. The throw went well wide, but the spell did its job. The blur curved in midair and careened away in the direction the sedan had fled.

"Nice job," said Nariko, dusting herself off and walking closer. "They took quite a gamble..."

The rest of Nariko's words grew tinny and distant as the cold wave emanating from the bite on Heath's neck swept over him. The world vanished in a crust of blue.

3

———

As Heath found his way toward consciousness, he felt as though he were lying inside a volcano, with only a thin layer of asbestos keeping the lava from burning him to ash. Oddly, he smelled something sweet and woodsy, that for some reason reminded him of Grandma's kitchen.

He could hear the lava sloshing around him in the darkness. Sounded awfully thin for lava. Pictures and film clips always made it look viscous, and thick as molasses.

Sometime later Heath realized he'd passed out again. That smell was still there, and now he heard the gentle plucking of a stringed instrument. Not a guitar though. And the lava felt less like lava. Cooler. Except on his face and neck. Hot hot hot in those places.

No. Wait. Only a line on his left cheek. And a spot at the back of his neck.

His eyes were gummy, but trying over and over proved he could blink them open.

Heath was naked, in a bathtub. He could tell that much through the bright, blurry world around him. Salmon and sand colored shapes that must have been tiles on walls and a floor. He rubbed his fingers together in the ... water? Apparently he'd been in the tub a long time. Long enough to go from grape to raisin.

"Awake. But not yet present."

A woman's voice. Familiar. Not Nariko, though her inflection reminded him of Nariko. This woman sounded ... more experienced. Not so much that she sounded older. More like the woman speaking had more depth to her soft voice.

"W-w-w-where..." Heath's jaw chattered too much to get any more of the sentence out, but the woman understood.

"Insensible. As I thought. And still so far out of balance." A single clucking sound. "More incense."

Those last two words weren't directed at Heath. He could tell that much. And there was something familiar about the pattern of tiles, but the connection felt elusive in his head. Every time he almost grasped it, some note of the music distracted him, or some undercurrent of the floral smell reminded him of vanilla, or his stomach rumbled.

All hope of comprehension was lost when the woman began speaking Japanese to someone else.

A second voice answered, also in Japanese. Nariko. Heath was sure of it. He'd know her voice anywhere, even when the world was blurry and hot and cold and...

Everything clicked. The tiles around this bathtub. Heath *had* seen them before. And that woman Nariko was talking to. She had the same inflection style because she taught Nariko to speak.

Heath tried in vain to cover himself with his hands.

"I'm-m-m-m s-s-s-s-orry to-to-to in-t-t-trude, Miss-s-s-sus—"

"Oh, stop," said Nariko's mother. "Bad enough you drag my daughter into your troubles. Don't make me listen to you try to talk in your current condition."

"Mother!"

"If you had left him to die, you would be free of him. Didn't you once tell me that was what you wanted more than—"

"Out! I can handle it from here."

"This is delicate work." Real reluctance in her tone. "Don't let him soil my bathroom because you are impatient."

"Go. Please."

"All right, but if you stocked your apartment properly you wouldn't need my bathroom in the first place..."

Mercifully, Nariko's mother switched to Japanese as she left the room, sparing Heath from understanding what further complaints she lodged.

Nariko knelt beside the tub and drew a pattern in front of Heath's face with the smoke of three incense sticks. Sandalwood and vanilla smoke. She moved on to other patterns over his body while whispering in Japanese. Prayers to her ancestors maybe.

The smoke swirled and shifted so hard the tub started spinning. Or maybe it was the room. Or maybe it was Heath. He wasn't quite sure, because the only thing he knew for certain was that he blinked and Nariko wasn't there.

The water was cooler now. Tepid. And the room didn't smell like sandalwood and vanilla. More like cherry and dragon's blood.

Had he passed out again?

Heath blinked and rubbed his eyes. The bathroom around him sharpened into view. The tile work. The black line art image of a bird in flight against a white mountain background. A photograph of Mr. and Mrs. Tachibana, smiling, standing at the peak of Mount Sobo in runner's gear.

Next to the bathtub a toilet and bidet. Fluffy, sage-colored towels and hand towels and washcloths hanging on the wall between the tub and a shower stall. Pedestal sink, currently ringed with a half-dozen white pillar candles, all lit and all half burned away.

No sign of the incense sticks. What Heath smelled must simply have been lingering in the air.

No sign of Heath's clothes, either. Though his backpack rested against the bottom of the sink's pedestal.

Heath gingerly ran his fingers over the cut on his cheek. Some kind of paste was smeared on it. Slightly tacky, but not enough to come away on his fingers at so light a touch. That spot on the back of his neck was covered with a bandage. Not a simple Band-Aid either. A small pad taped into place, and when he pressed on it Heath could feel a sharp warning that pressing on it was a bad idea. He could also feel that herbs and perhaps another paste had been applied under the bandage.

He stood, water dripping off his waterlogged frame. His knees felt shaky, and he steadied himself with a hand on the wall to help himself out of the tub. A tremor shook his stomach hard enough to suggest he hadn't eaten in days. But more important than that was stepping to the toilet to relieve himself.

When he washed up, he got his first good look in the mirror. His skin looked downright pale. Girlfriends always liked to describe his skin tone as light milk chocolate. But the way he looked right now, someone had gone heavy on the milk and light on the cocoa beans.

His eyes looked good though. He'd expected them to be bloodshot.

Heath sat cross-legged on the cold, wet tile floor and dug into his backpack. First he pulled out the bedpan, his mini saucepan incense censer. Next the symbol and sigil covered three-inch-by-three-inch cherry wood box that housed travel packs of his own incenses. From there, he dug out another dozen herbs and not quite half as many oils.

Whatever that red blur had done to Heath, either the bite or the cure had stripped him of all his casual protection magics. And there was no way he was leaving this bathroom without getting every one of them back in place.

And since it looked as though some pretty serious players were coming after him, maybe it was time to add a few extras.

THE FIRST TIME HEATH HAD SEEN NARIKO'S BEDROOM IN HER PARENTS' house, she'd had soccer and J-pop posters on the walls, clothes on the floor, and makeup and books scattered everywhere. Half a grilled cheese sandwich had awaited her attention on top of her nightstand alarm clock with its giant red numbers. The whole room had smelled like jasmine and sandalwood. Her father had said she'd "exploded" home from college for spring break.

That was five years ago, when neither Heath nor Nariko was old enough to drink.

The room around Heath right now fit in better with the décor of the rest of the house. Cream-colored carpet with precision vacuum lines. Professional paint job on the walls in a light canary yellow. Delicate golden curtains framing the second-story view of Douglas firs instead of Nariko's old blackout drapes banishing it. And a brand new queen mattress with a teak frame, dead center of the room instead of shoved along one wall where she used to keep the old one.

Each of the three interior walls now had a single line art painting of a Japanese countryside, as though depicting the view in three directions from the peak of a mountain. The only sound Heath could hear was the tinkling of a wooden wind chime outside the window.

Nariko perched on the edge of the bed, watching Heath take it all in. She was still wearing the shirt and slacks combo from Tsarina's, so it must have been the same day. Made Heath feel better that he was still wearing the same black jeans and blue-and-white striped shirt.

"No bookshelves," he said finally. "No nightstands. Not even a chest of drawers."

"I'm welcome to sleep here anytime I like. But Mom wouldn't want me thinking I could move back in."

"Thank you."

Nariko looked away, fiddled with the duvet. "I told you. You're too pretty to be a corpse."

Heath thought about saying more. About her mother, about how much he understood or thought he understood about what Nariko had brought on herself by bringing him here. But the moment was ruined when his stomach rumbled hard enough to shake his knees.

"Reminds me," said Nariko. "Your *pirozhkis* are in the fridge. Inga had them sent here."

Heath let that sink in for a moment. Inga had said she'd send the food to his place, but instead it found Heath down here in a suburb along the southwest border of town. Heath had never picked up any magic at Tsarina's, either, which made the food delivery even spookier. But thinking about that that made Heath realize something.

"Did you get me all the way here on the back of your bike?"

"Like I had another option? You're heavier than you look, by the way. I'd for—Made for an awkward ride, let me tell you."

"It's a comical image," Heath said, fighting a smile. "From downtown to Lake Oswego…"

"Would be if you weren't dying at the time." All business in her eyes again. "Any idea what that red thing was?"

"Didn't get a good look, but I'm betting it was a snapper."

Nariko fluttered her lashes in that way that clearly meant, "and that is…"

"When some of the old world witches came to the United States from Spain and Italy, their magic changed to accommodate the new world. They started finding new spirits to work with, new combinations—"

"Should I be taking notes?"

"Fine. Between logging and gold mining, the mass migration west in the nineteenth century drove two breeds of woodpeckers to extinction. The snapper is a bird spirit who's pissed about that and out for revenge. Bind one and you can give it targets."

Nariko stared at Heath, one eyebrow slowly ascending to an arch. When it reached its apex she said, "Are you telling me you were almost killed by a dead, homicidal woodpecker?"

"Who the Hell would admit that if it weren't true?"

"Fair point." Nariko shrugged. "What's it got to do with Spain and Italy?"

"Nothing, except that those were the immigrant witches who first discovered and bound snappers. And the I.D.s had Italian last names despite the decidedly un-Italian first names. Figured it was a statement."

"Reminds me." Nariko snapped her fingers. "Guy with the submachine gun. He was a distraction, wasn't he?"

"Yeah, I think so." Heath scratched around the edges of the tape on the back of his neck. "Had some kind of *look-at-me* spell on his trench coat, same as the two from the parking lot."

"Marvin and Jarvis. And *don't pick at that.*"

Heath lowered his hands. "Point is, they they got us out of the building and someplace open where the snapper could strike while all our attention was on the guys in trench coats. It's a theory, anyway."

"So now what?"

Heath shook his head. "I knew getting this book was going to be tricky, but I didn't think anyone would be actively trying to kill me for it. I won't hold it against you if you want out."

Nariko sighed. "You heard that little dig from my mom, didn't you?"

Heath sucked in his lips to keep from answering.

"I don't want you dead." She wouldn't look at him. She was watching the dark clouds rolling through the skies out the window. "I never did. Not really. I just wanted..."

"You don't have to do this."

She looked at him then, too much feeling in her green eyes for Heath to interpret it all.

"I'm not going to let you get killed because no one corporeal is watching your back."

"If anyone's going to kill me it'll be you?"

That got a smirk out of her. "You're never going to let me live that one down, are you?"

"I still can't decide if you meant it as a sideways compliment or a sideways insult."

"Both." She stood and folded her arms. "And you never answered my question. Now what?"

"I need answers. Some idea what I'm dealing with. Back at my place I can—"

"I know you're good at not being followed when you put your mind to it, but if you think your place isn't being watched – or maybe even actively under assault – then you're too stupid to live and I withdraw my protection."

Not even a hint of humor in her posture.

"Fine. No choice then. I need to see the Sybil."

"I wouldn't call her reliable."

"I've got three trapped spirits back at my place that could get me the answers I need in an hour. But if you think going there's a bad idea, I don't see what my options are."

"Your cards can't help here?" She pointed to Heath's backpack. "You can't tell me you don't have a deck tucked away somewhere inside that beast."

"I do, but they'd be no more use than cowrie shells. Not for this."

"Ouija board maybe?"

"Nariko."

"Fine, but I'm waiting by the bike and keeping watch for this one."

———

THE *PIROZHKIS* FULL OF EGGS, POTATOES AND BACON HELPED SETTLE Heath's stomach, and Nariko's mother insisted to Nariko that he also have a cup of oolong tea and two cold, hard boiled eggs, unsalted.

By the time Heath finished eating, he had to admit he felt better. More aware of his surroundings when he followed Nariko out through the garage to where her BMW was parked on the cobblestone driveway in front of an emerald green Lexus SUV. She swung her leg over the bike, but before he got on behind her he stopped and looked up and down the street.

Or at least what he could see of it. Her parents lived near the top of a hill, so the road curved sharply away one direction and sharply down in the other. The borders between their house and their neighbors' were demarcated with eight-foot-tall arborvitae shrubs, hemming his view still further. Elms and Douglas firs lined the other side of the street, protecting those who lived below from feeling looked-down upon.

Heath closed his physical eyes and let himself see with his spirit eyes. First thing he picked up was that big presence inside the hill itself, like a sleeping giant caught mid-dream. But Heath always saw the giant when he was here, and though its sleep was sometimes restless, it never yet woke up that he'd heard of. Thing was so big it freaked him out on his first visit, but apparently the spirit had something to do with Shugendō.

Other than that, not much more to see except a couple of plant sprites tending to what they considered theirs. No watchers. No servitors. No little ghosties running around, keeping an eye on him for someone else. At least, not just at that time.

"Mom may not like you," said Nariko, "but she'd give my baby sister up for adoption before she'd let anyone spy on a guest in her house."

Heath nodded, but wasn't ready to mount the bike yet. The wind was stronger now, chilly in the late afternoon. It tousled his hair, and spread the smell of evergreen from the arborvitae and fresh cut grass from the lawn.

He opened his eyes. Up above the storm clouds persisted. That just wasn't normal.

"Anything on the news about that?" Heath asked, pointing up.

"It's not coming in from the sea and it's not blowing down from Canada. Apparently its supposed to be gone by now. The T.V. meteorologists keep saying we're due to hit the nineties with clear skies anytime now. But the pressure keeps dropping anyway. I tucked a couple of jackets under the seat for us, just in case."

Heath nodded. He'd have to ask the Sybil about the weather. But first, something else took priority.

"Do you still have that other guy's I.D.? Jarvis?"

"Laid some smack down with it while you were out. Not sure I reached him though."

So much for Heath's first-line-of-defense thought.

"With any luck the snapper got them both." Heath looked at the tight bun still holding back all of Nariko's hair. "Can you spare any—"

She fished a nail pairing out of her pocket. "Had a feeling you'd ask for a strand of hair or something. Your magic is so…"

"Practical?"

"Physical."

"I'll take it," he said. He pulled a piece of white chalk from his shirt pocket, then hesitated. "Think your mom would mind if I used her front walk for—"

"You so want to use public land for this."

Heath walked out to the city-owned sidewalk and Nariko walked her bike behind him. He spat onto the concrete, and put Nariko's nail clipping in the tiny puddle.

"Ever the romantic," she said, and he hushed her.

He drew a circle around the spit and paring. Then he drew three circles around that, and seven circles around those. He fished a vial of confusion oil out of his backpack, and poured a drop in every one of those circles.

Next he licked his finger and tested the wind, gauging its exact strength and direction. He dug out a little ground cinnamon mixed with marjoram, comfrey, and a touch of a couple of other things he wouldn't admit to. Heath dried off his finger, took a generous pinch of the mixture and whispered to it. He moved his hand around until it was in the right spot so that as he rubbed his fingertips together, the powder scattered in the wind all over each of the circles and outside them besides.

He shook his fist in the direction of the wind and said, with all the force he could muster, "You call the wrong man bald-head and those bears are going to get you. See if they don't."

Nariko laughed, but Heath held his focus. He spat left, then right, then clapped his hands hard three times.

"There," he said, putting away his confusion oil and powder. "Since your mom gave us breathing room, that should buy us at least a few hours."

Nariko was still chuckling. "I can just picture your old mentor teaching you that spell. He was bald, right? Tell me he was bald."

"No one taught me that one." Heath slung his backpack onto his shoulders. "Each of us conjure folk works a little differently."

"How is anyone supposed to take your magic seriously?" She shook her head. "I felt power move, but I mean, come on. Bald head?"

"That's what you get for being an ancestor-worshiping pagan. No idea how much power there is in the Good Book, nor what you can do with it when you get creative."

Heath mounted the bike behind Nariko and slipped his arms around her waist. She adjusted in her seat, and it felt like she was snuggling in. But she couldn't have been. Not anymore.

"That was from the Bible? Bald head?"

"And the bears." Heath kept his smile inside and gave her a solemn nod. "Look it up."

***

THE SYBIL OF PORTLAND WASN'T GREEK. IF ANYTHING, SHE LOOKED eastern European. And she didn't spend all day in a cave inhaling weird vapors. Frankly, all things considered, Heath thought her title was false advertising.

And despite all the lovely spots in nature parks around Portland she could have chosen from, she had to position herself the way she might have in Manhattan or New Orleans – downtown. She took up her post between the Plaza Blocks, in the middle of nearly everything.

But then, Heath supposed that everyone had to make a living, and her current location certainly drew foot traffic.

The Plaza Blocks were green grass parks lined with old elm and ginko trees. They had statues and enough history that it was common to see some troop of kids meandering along while their wranglers tried to impart knowledge about this event or what used to happen on that spot. The parks also had plenty of benches, where couples could enjoy a nice day while all around them birds sang and fat squirrels frolicked. And businesspeople from the public and private office buildings all around could come and tell themselves they were getting fresh air while bolting down their lunches over hurried phone calls.

But then, Heath didn't have to watch them to know he would never have survived a life of office work. That path had been closed to him years ago.

No googly-eyed lovers or crowds of schoolkids today, and the office-types carrying briefcases or deli sandwiches or take-out bags of Korean barbecue quick-stepped through the growing wind on their way back to their offices.

Locals could smell rain on the air, and they all wanted to be inside when it broke. Which meant they had more sense than Heath, but he knew that already.

More sense than the Sybil too, it seemed. She stood in her normal place on the double-wide sidewalk of Main Street, just beside the spot where traffic had to part around the big bronze stag and its octagonal concrete base that combined to form Elk Fountain, there in the middle of the street.

To avoid advertising her true calling – or maybe just to make a buck in between seekers – the five-foot-six-inch Sybil posed as a human statue of a stage magician. Her skin, short hair, and tuxedo were painted a shimmering blue-silver. She held a matching top hat in one hand and a wand in the other.

Heath had to admit that, for a human statue, she had a pretty good bit. If anyone walked up and put regular money in the hat, she would smile, incline her head, wave her wand in three circles and tap the hat. A blue-silver felt rabbit would poke its head up, then withdraw and disappear.

Of course, the money vanished too. Anyone who looked into the hat wouldn't see their money or the rabbit. But they could see the trick again if they threw in some more cash.

Human statues weren't common in Portland, so even under the threatening skies Heath had to wait for three white boys who wore polo shirts with the collars up to throw quarters in her hat. While they watched her routine, they speculated loudly about how she did it. Heath was just about at the point of performing a little go-away magic when they finally cleared off on their own.

Heath looked back at Nariko, waiting for him at the corner with her bike idling. She didn't meet his eye, though. She was too busy keeping watch.

Heath approached the Sybil. He held up a silver dollar, tapped the hand she held her hat with, and dropped the coin in her hat. He said, "I can still tell Suit to go fuck himself. He substantially misrepresented the risk level. But if I do, it puts me in a financial bind. Am I better off keeping or breaking his deal?"

The Sybil smiled and inclined her head. She waved her wand once. She spoke in a hollow, distant voice without moving her lips.

"Keep his deal and you must find Death. Break his deal and Death will find you first."

"Well doesn't that just sound lovely? Maybe Nariko's got a point about you." Heath grimaced. "If I seek the book, what opposition should concern me most?"

Another pass of the wand.

"The book itself."

"Oh, fucking wonderful. What's the best way for me to survive this mess?"

A final pass of the wand. The Sybil tapped her hat, and up popped the rabbit. And Heath would have sworn the hollow voice came from the rabbit when he heard the Sybil say, "Your only future lies through your past."

Heath closed his eyes and gritted his teeth. A thousand things he could have been doing right now, and here he stood listening to cryptic bullshit. Had he really believed she would tell him to blow town? Give him some excuse to drive down the coast with Nariko until the whole thing blew over?

Not that Nariko was likely to go with him, even if the Sybil suggested it. *Especially* if the Sybil suggested it.

He hadn't even remembered to ask about the weather.

Heath opened his eyes and let out a slow sigh through his nose. He stretched his lips in as close to a smile as he could give the Sybil while he fished a five dollar bill out of his pocket. Strictly speaking, tipping the Sybil wasn't necessary. But Heath believed that tips made the world go round.

"Thank you," he said, and gave her the five.

The Sybil went through her routine, and Heath forced himself to watch out of politeness. His feet itched to return to Nariko's bike and get back to work. But when the rabbit popped up something happened that Heath had never heard of happening before.

The Sybil spoke without answering a question.

Again the hollow voice seemed to come from the rabbit. It said, "If you do not find the book, your death will be the first. Nariko's the second. And many others will follow."

4

"OH, BULLSHIT!" SAID NARIKO. "THE SYBIL DID *NOT* MENTION ME by name."

In just about any other downtown restaurant, that outburst would have drawn curious looks from the other patrons. But at Foxy, even at only half-full, it slipped past the other diners unnoticed.

Most likely because Heath and Nariko were having the least intriguing conversation in earshot. Without even trying, Heath had learned that the middle-aged gay couple at the next booth were having difficulties with their S&M arrangement, and that at least two of the loud young women at a nearby four-top were sure their lovers were cheating. Possibly together.

But then, Heath had never been in Foxy without hearing conversations like these. Drama seemed built into the foundation.

Foxy looked less like a diner than the aftermath of an explosion in a drag queen's dressing room. Up high the walls were covered in boas and feather masks, single velvet gloves on ceramic arms, Styrofoam heads in full makeup propping up outrageous wigs, and some articles of costuming that Heath couldn't quite puzzle out.

Lower down were posters from movies like *Faster Pussycat, Kill, Kill* and fliers from twenty years of local drag shows. Heath was sitting on the thrice-patched brown vinyl of a booth seat with broken springs, under a framed poster from *To Wong Foo, Thanks for Everything, Julie Newmar,* signed by the stars, the director and the writer. All over the walls at head height were autographed black-and-white photos of movie stars and drag show legends.

The place smelled like coffee, scrambled eggs, and talcum powder. The black-and-white checkered floor always looked a little grimy, and so did the staff, but the food was good. Even while she complained, Nariko hacked her links of chicken apple sausage into tiny bites and stuffed one in her mouth.

"I wouldn't lie to you about the Sybil," said Heath, swirling his too-hot coffee in its chipped blue mug. "You would have heard her if you'd—"

"Uh uh." Nariko shook her head. "You're not going to convince me with that you-weren't-there garbage. The Sybil doesn't name names. Never does. Titles, sometimes, if they're sufficiently obfuscated to fit her style. She once referred to my mother as the Queen of the Mountain and you as the Digger of Fate."

"Wait. *You* consulted the Sybil? When was this?"

"Doesn't matter. Point is, naming names is like giving useful answers. The Sybil just isn't capable of it."

Heath thought about that while he added more sugar to his coffee and sipped. Just right.

"What about the rest of it? Death and so on? You don't think her warning has merit, even if it's a little difficult to interpret?"

Nariko jabbed a bite of sausage in the air to punctuate her words. "Difficult to interpret is putting it mildly. Bitch once told me I would never reach my full power until 'the Queen found her rest under the Mountain.'"

Heath sucked in his lips and got very interested in the remains of his cheddar scrambled eggs, trying to scrape some of the leftover cheddar onto his fork.

"Yeah, yeah," said Nariko around a bite of sausage. "But you don't understand. Mom's never going to die."

Heath dropped his silverware and looked up at Nariko. Her green eyes were shiny with unshed tears.

"You say that like it's not only true, but it's a bad thing."

Nariko blinked, and her eyes were all business again.

"Never mind that. So the Sybil says lots of people are going to die unless you find Saint Sippy's Nasty Journal."

Heath still stared at Nariko, trying to see answers somewhere in her face, but she shook her head. It was only the barest movement, scant fractions of an inch, but it was enough for Heath to get the message.

Heath popped the rest of his melted cheese in his mouth and said, "Yeah, but she didn't give me any hints about anything useful, like where it might be or what kind of death we're talking about."

"Yes, she did," said Colin, slipping into the booth beside Nariko and forcing her to wedge in close to the wall. She was too slack-jawed with shock at his sudden appearance to object, and Heath couldn't blame her.

Sudden appearance was right. One moment Colin wasn't there, the next he was just standing beside their booth, worn jeans, Iron Maiden tour shirt and all.

"I wasn't nearby when you met the Sybil, but if you remembered right when you quoted her—"

"*Where the hell did you come from?*"

Heath wasn't sure if he asked that, or Nariko did, or if the shock of Colin's appearance synchronized them into one of their old couple moments.

Colin snickered, and again Heath thought of a cartoon dog.

"I told you guys. I found a real invisibility spell in one of those old books. You have to set it up in advance, but then you just need to carry the amulet" – Colin held up a small, laminated square of paper featuring an ornate drawing inside a circle – "and activate it."

Colin looked at them both. "Won't work while you're watching me though."

"I know," Heath said slowly, "at least sixteen ways to go about unobserved, unseen or ignored, but real invisibility? The kind that hides you even when someone's staring at you as close as arm's reach?" Heath shuddered like someone walked over his grave. "That's some scary shit."

"It's got its uses." Colin snatched up an abandoned slice of wheat toast from Heath's plate. "But about what the Sybil said—"

"Budge over," said Nariko. She looked at how much seat she had and how much Colin had, then fixed him with the look she used to banish unwanted admirers.

Colin scooted to the edge of the seat.

"What are you doing here?" said Heath. "I thought you were out."

"I felt bad about that," said Colin with a mouthful of toast. He swigged from Nariko's untouched water glass. "Both of you have pulled me out of a few jams. Not right for me to turn tail when you're in trouble. So I did a little digging on my own and figured I'd catch up with you later."

"But how did you find us?" Heath shook his head. "I know I got that spell right."

"You did. No doubt. When I tried to find you guys with magic the spell went haywire. Tried to claim you were maybe a dozen different places all at once." Colin shrugged. "So I relied on what I know of you guys."

He twirled a finger to indicate their surroundings. "This place is your comfort food, especially when you're together. Anyway, if I'm right about what the Sybil said..."

Colin looked from Heath to Nariko and back, making sure he wasn't going to be interrupted.

"The book itself is dangerous. Like Lovecraft and *Evil Dead* dangerous."

"You of all people should know that books are books," said Heath. "Same as herbs are herbs. Give our stuff to almost anyone in this diner and they couldn't magic up enough power to blow a lightbulb. Takes talent. Takes training."

"Initiations help too," said Nariko, then gave a grudging nod to Colin. "For some of us, anyway."

"Hey, my books include initiations. They just don't call them that.

They use phrases like 'activation sequence' or 'meeting the spirits.' Stuff like that."

"Point is," said Heath, taking a sip of coffee, "how can a book be dangerous?"

"Well, we're not exactly talking about the Avon *Necronomicon* here, mass-published and perfect-bound." Colin stuffed the rest of that piece of toast in his mouth. "'s one of a kind."

"A talisman as well as a grimoire," said Nariko to Heath. "Makes sense."

Colin cut in before Heath could reply.

"Not jusht a talisman." Colin swallowed. "Everyone agrees that Saint Cyprian was a magical badass before he came up against God" — Colin drew out the name of the Almighty as though he were a southern televangelist — "lost, and saw the light. But some of the stories about Saint Cyprian say that the day he decided to convert, he – how did they put it? – 'thrust his evil inside his tome and cast it into the fire.'"

"Let me guess." Heath set down his cup. "Book didn't burn."

"Apparently he threw the book in the fire and left. Didn't think to check on it. But after his first confession, the Father Confessor, a Jesuit, sent a novitiate monk to see what became of the grimoire. The hearth had burned itself out but the book was intact, not just the cover but every page crisp as the day it was tanned."

"Tanned?" said Nariko.

"Sheepskin," said Colin.

"You found all this out online?"

"I can't reveal my sources." Colin grinned like a sailor on leave reaching the steps of a whorehouse.

Heath smiled. "And here I thought you abandoned us."

"He'll wish he had," said the older gay man at the next booth as he stood and faced the trio. Just the start of crow's feet and smile lines on the man's tanned face, and his short black hair was slicked straight back.

But his eye sockets were empty, and small fires burned where his eyes should have been.

"WHAT ARE YOU DOING, *PAPI*?" SAID THE YOUNGER GAY MAN, HIS VOICE hinting at a Puerto Rican accent. He stood up and put his hand on Fire Eyes' shoulder. This younger guy had to have been at least twenty-eight, but his Latin skin was so smooth he looked like he didn't need to shave.

Now the other patrons of Foxy were paying attention. Even the dingy wait staff stopped busing tables to watch. Occult discussions might not have raised an eyebrow, but a domestic situation? That could be fodder for a whole evening's entertainment.

Fire Eyes didn't care, and didn't seem to notice the hand on his shoulder.

"Heath Cyr," he said, voice lowering to a rumble on the edge of human hearing. Or at least on the edge of Heath's. "Vow before me that you shall abandon all claim to *The Black Book of Saint Cyprian* or never leave this place alive."

"No manners at all?" said Heath, his hand edging below the table and into his backpack. "Where I come from, mister, we introduce ourselves before we start flinging threats."

Nariko reached behind her to finger the single steel spike that held her bun in place. Colin only stared wide-eyed.

"You watch your mouth, boy," said the younger gay man, cracking his knuckles and stepping up just behind and left of Fire Eyes. "You're not so pretty I won't break your nose, you say the wrong thing."

Colin slipped under the table.

"Don't you break anything," called a woman from behind the counter. "I *will* call the police and they *will* come."

"*The Black Book* is a thing of darkness," said Fire Eyes, "and you are a thing of twilight. You have not the darkness nor the light to call forth its power. And this is your final warning. Swear now or suffer."

Heath hated fighting possessed people. But maybe with all the focus on him, Nariko or Colin could find the puppet-master pulling Fire Eyes' strings.

"Fine," said Heath, as his fingers found their grip on a frosted glass vial. "I'll swear."

Heath grinned. "Fuck. You."

Heath dove right and yanked the cork out of the vial with his teeth like he was pulling the pin on a grenade in some old war film.

Flames roared out of Fire Eyes' sockets, melting the seat behind Heath and setting fire to pictures and posters on the wall, as well as the wall itself.

People screamed.

Nariko swung the fist holding her steel spike. Punching, not stabbing. Her long black hair fell loose and wild past her shoulders.

Heath flung holy water in the face of Fire Eyes, shouting, "Brother Fox carried the Word!"

Nariko connected with Fire Eyes' jaw, a punch solid enough that Heath heard the *thunk* over the crackling of decorations catching fire. Apparently Foxy's décor was quite flammable. The heat spreading behind him was rapidly reaching sunburn-at-the-beach levels. Smoke roiled up above him. A fire alarm began a steady screech.

Fire Eyes staggered back a step, the blaze in his sockets diminished while all around Heath the fire spread further, smoke weaving around him.

"What the fuck, *Papi*?"

Heath rolled to his feet and immediately had to jump over another wash of eye-shot fire that burnt away whatever coated the tile floor. Not as much or as strong as the first wave, but the blaze it set stretched to connect to its kin behind him.

Sirens in the background now, and more screaming as patrons shoved and trampled their way out the front and the back, coughing as they wedged past. Out of the corner of his eye Heath could see a neckbeard in an apron running out of the kitchen, carrying a fire extinguisher. Neckbeard had a little white mask covering his mouth and nose, at least.

And Heath's pants were on fire. Terror seized him at the thought of burning alive. He started beating his legs with his backpack, hoping its enchantments would help put out the flames.

More fire behind him and to the left, hot enough that he was sweating before he knew it. Smoke everywhere now, Heath breathing through the collar of his sweaty t-shirt. Stampeding patrons to his right. And in front of him, Fire Eyes, trembling and swaying while the crying younger gay man tried fruitlessly to drag his lover out the door and away from the building inferno.

Nariko stood on her seat, holding her spike in both hands and chanting in rapid Japanese. Her hair floated as on a cushion of its own air. Smoke passed around her but didn't touch her. Heath could feel power rising from below.

Thump!

Heath couldn't see the source of the sound, but the moment he heard it Fire Eyes collapsed, the flames in his eye sockets giving way to dark brown eyes. But Heath could only catch a glimpse before Former-Fire-Eyes' lover dragged him out the door.

Through the growing haze of smoke Heath saw Colin, a brown growler clutched in both hands where he stood over an unconscious woman three tables away.

Neckbeard opened up on Heath's legs with the fire extinguisher, finishing what his backpack had started. Cold white spray. He then started on the fire itself.

"No!" yelled Heath. "Too late! Get out."

But Neckbeard elbowed Heath aside and swept his spray across the flames. He looked valiant but accomplished nothing.

"Go!" yelled Nariko, still untouched by flame or smoke.

Heath coughed, but pointed to the downed woman beside C— where Colin had been a moment ago. Colin had vanished again.

"I'll get her."

And Nariko turned into the spreading haze, which parted around whatever spell she had going. Heath had no such spell up himself, so he availed himself of the better part of valor. He wiped sweat from his forehead and shielded his face against the intense heat on his way into the crowded street.

And that street was *crowded*. None of the patrons had left. They were all watching the flames, or crying and holding each other, or taking pictures or videos, or talking on their phones. And it wasn't just the patrons. Enough people were gathering that the fire engines and ambulances up the block had someone yelling into a megaphone to get the attention their blaring sirens weren't. News vans were right behind them, and overhead Heath thought he saw the shadow of a helicopter. Maybe two.

Police officers pushed through the crowd, desperate to exert some control.

A heavy-set woman in a Foxy t-shirt and black jeans was yelling at Former-Fire-Eyes and his lover. But Former-Fire-Eyes was dazed and the lover was yelling back in Spanish. They had a crowd of their own forming.

Heath stood there shaking from his ankles up, singed and sweaty. Shock began laying a comfy blanket over his stress and strain. Everything felt just a little too distant. Even the bird pecking at his shoulder.

Bird? There was no bird when Heath brushed at his shoulder, but the pecking began again.

No. Not pecking. Tapping. A finger tapping.

Heath turned. There was Colin. Looking hazy, like he was still in the smoke. Weird Colin with his weird magic self-help books like *The Amazing Miracle of Horus Power* and *The Irresistible Force of Swami Magic*. Colin was hushing him. Why?

"Come on." Colin whispered, but Heath could hear him clear as a bell. He took Heath by the hand and led him down the street.

"But Nariko…" Heath's voice sounded funny in his ears. Distant. Almost tinny.

"I'll get her next."

Colin led Heath through the crowd and no one noticed them. Heath felt like he'd cast an *ain't-your-problem* spell, the kind that made people notice everything but him unless he did something obnoxious or got in their faces.

Then Colin was opening the front passenger door of his little white Saturn sedan and settling Heath onto the seat.

"Be right back," said Colin, and as he hustled off, it occurred to

Heath that the world was too distant. That he shouldn't be feeling his way through a thick blanket of cotton.

Someone had just tried to kill him.

There. A flare of feeling. Heat in the muffle. Heath shook his head and dug through his backpack for some fresh yellow rue leaves and their green berry middles. Took longer than it should have. Felt like he was wearing winter gloves.

But he found that rue. He held up a big pinch and made the sign of the cross over it three times. Then he said, "Wake me up, Uncle Loko. Wake me up now. Bad time to be sleeping."

He chewed the bitter rue and felt the world rush back in. Jitters all through his bones and dancing in his stomach. Sweaty, hot and feverish everywhere, except cold at the back of his neck, and sticky where the fire extinguisher got him.

But that rush came in and eased on through so smoothly that Heath could almost feel Uncle Loko rubbing the sore spot on the back of his neck, making everything better. But even Uncle Loko wasn't *that* good a doctor. With a little bitter rue, Uncle Loko could settle him right down, but everything in Heath's world was far from all right.

But now, at least, he could assess himself.

Heath probably had burns on his shins and calves, but they weren't screaming at him, so they could wait. Heath's jeans were singed pretty badly from the knees to the cuffs, but not his shoes. Which made no sense whatsoever, unless it was a sign from Papa Legba telling him to run.

But somehow, Heath doubted that.

The rear driver-side door opened and Heath damn near wrenched his neck spinning to see, but it was Nariko dropping down onto the seat, angry enough to chew coal and spit diamonds.

"Gone!" she snapped, as Colin opened his own door and jumped into the driver's seat. "Paramedics snatched her before I could ask a single question."

"We'll figure it out," said Heath. "But not here."

"Don't worry." Colin held up a small handful of red-brown hair. "I cut off a hunk, just in case. Seemed like your kind of thing, Heath."

Heath smiled.

Colin revved the engine to a mild cough. "Let's roll."

HEATH HAD BEEN TO COLIN'S PLACE SIX TIMES NOW, AND IT SURPRISED him every time. He kept expecting Colin to live like a typical college student – in a dorm, maybe, or at least a one-room studio with a stack of pizza boxes in the corner and more books than bookshelves. Someplace that smelled like nag champa and burnt coffee.

He certainly did not expect the kind of two-bedroom condo that looked like it should belong to a Yuppie. Carpeting the color of sea foam with a pale blue couch, loveseat, and pair of recliners. Wall mounted forty-inch television with surround sound speakers set into the walls. A walnut coffee table with fanned magazines about architecture as well as music. Abstract oil paintings on the walls, alive with rainbow colors, all the work of local artists. On a stand in the corner waited an acoustic guitar that Heath suspected was worth more than Colin's Saturn.

The place smelled like homemade potpourri. Heath could pick out mint, geranium, rose, and lemon verbena.

And that didn't even include the fancy dining room, or the elegant kitchen with its cherry hardwood floor and swirls of blue and pink through its white marble counters.

The bedrooms were upstairs, though one had been converted into a music studio, where Colin housed the rest of his guitars as well as his recording equipment.

Nariko couldn't get a step inside the cherry wood entryway before commenting.

"Way too much style for a straight man."

"Nothing wrong with knowing what you like," said Colin, gazing fondly over his furniture. "And who said I was straight?"

"I can't wear anything low-cut around you without you practically drooling. Even my form fitting tops—"

"What can I say?" asked Colin with a shrug. "You have a great rack, and I'm an equal opportunity lover."

"I hate to interrupt," said Heath, "but we do have more pressing matters than who Colin sleeps with."

"Whom," said Colin.

"Whomever." Heath strode past them, heading for the kitchen. His grip tight on the hair from the unconscious woman at Foxy. Nariko and Colin followed as soon as they locked the door behind them.

Heath began setting up on the marble center island, first separating the woman's red-brown hairs into two piles, one twice as big as the other. Then he dug through his backpack for the bedpan, his incense, dollar-store matches, and a few other things.

And while he prepared, he had questions for Colin, who was grabbing Teufelsbrau IPAs for himself and Nariko, who perched on a counter behind Heath.

"I know the coincidental timing of your knocking out that woman with the collapse of Fire Eyes is compelling, but how certain are you that she conjured that spirit?"

"Positive," said Colin, popping the cap off his beer. "She had the intense look. She was mumbling..."

Colin sipped from his beer, and Heath turned and folded his arms across his chest. He shot Colin an irritated grin, knowing that part of the answer was still coming.

"Oh, yeah," said Colin. "And she was the only patron in the restaurant with a sigil from the *Grimoire of Pope Honorius* sketched out in salt on her table."

"How do you know that's what it was?"

"Just because I don't *use* the magic in those books doesn't mean I don't *read* them. They're *fascinating*."

"Colin?" said Nariko.

"Yeah?"

"I'm glad you're on our side."

"Feeling's mutual."

They clinked beers and toasted each other.

Heath was about to ask another question, but Colin cut in as though finishing his comment to Nariko. "And not just 'cause you're hot."

Nariko turned to say something, but Heath cleared his throat. She shook her head dismissively and looked away. Heath looked back at Colin.

"Did she ever get a look at you?"

"Nope," said Colin. "That's why I figure we're safe here. My own safeguards notwithstanding, I figure we're better off where they shouldn't be looking for us."

"Makes sense," said Heath, tilting his head in thought. "You were seen abandoning us earlier—"

"And you vanished under the table at the first sign of trouble," finished Nariko. She turned to Heath. "We should be good as long as your bald-head spell holds out."

"Bald-head spell?" said Colin.

"Pagans," said Heath, shaking his head as he turned and opened his portable censer, "the bedpan." He tossed a small round coal onto the bed of salt, which was dirty from previous uses, but pure enough for his purposes. He lit the coal with dollar store matches and turned back. "And that spell should hold off any interested parties until about midnight."

"I've got some pretty solid wards against magical traces," said Colin, "plus a couple of watchdog spirits keeping an eye on things. Oh, and I'm an agnostic, thank you. I don't know why any of this shit works. I'm just glad it does."

"You just admitted you deal with spirits," said Nariko. "How can you call yourself agnostic? Shouldn't you at least call yourself an animist?"

"What *is* a spirit?" countered Colin. "How do I know these aren't aspects of my own mind—"

Heath cleared his throat again.

"Do you need a beer?" asked Colin with exaggerated innocence. "You sound parched."

"We have a small supply of hair here. Enough for probably one good spell and one longer-term enchantment."

"Puppet work?" Nariko's face brightened. "I love watching you do puppet work."

"Poppet," corrected Heath, "and before we get to that we need to make sure we're all on the same page here."

"Why did Fire Eyes give you two chances to back off before attacking?" asked Nariko, who then finished her beer.

"Exactly." Heath blew out a slow breath. "Whoever called up Fire Eyes couldn't be working with the guys from Tsarina's. They were all about distraction to set up their attack. Fire Eyes wanted my word to back off, and even gave me a bullshit reason."

"Might not be bullshit," said Colin. "The purists out there would say you use your share of black magic – maybe more than your share – which means she might have seen you as a potential ally, long term." Colin shrugged. "Also the *Black Book* might just be the kind of thing that corrupts whatever it touches."

"But why warn me off?"

"Me, I find the prospect of you going full-dark kind of scary. But her?" Colin tipped back his beer. "I don't know. Ex-lover? She was pretty cute. Even had green eyes like Nariko here."

"Didn't recognize her," said Heath, shaking his head.

Nariko fetched her own second beer, and the things she didn't say felt all too loud to Heath.

"So we have one more mystery there. My landlord wants me to fetch this book. Some karcist-style sorcerer woman was willing to warn me off, but then went straight to lethal force when I objected. And a third group with vaguely Italian connections tried to kill me just to keep me 'out of the equation.'"

"Suddenly I'm rethinking the wisdom of having you as a house guest," said Colin, returning to his brushed steel refrigerator for a second IPA.

"My rep can't be that big. Not these days. Not after that Vizinha stuff."

"What happened there anyway?" asked Nariko. "Another angry ex-?"

"You're more her style," said Colin. "Though I'd be happy to introduce her to the joys of men, if she ever got curious."

"She's not an ex-," said Heath, "and the official story was she lost a couple of clients to me and decided to show me up. Now those clients won't touch either of us." Heath shook his head. "But if you want to go out with her Colin, give it a shot. She likes guys as much as girls. Just don't tell me about it, and don't force us to be in the same place at the same time. Results wouldn't be pretty."

"Yeah," said Nariko, "heard about your little Spaghetti Western moment at Gripper." Nariko rolled her bottle back and forth in her hands. "Think she's got anything to do with this?"

"Can't rule it out. The woman embraces spite the way some women embrace fashion. And she did say something about not wanting to 'raise a dead issue.'"

"So we know something about the competition," said Colin, but before he could continue, Heath cut in.

"Wait. Colin. You heard something in the Sybil's words that I missed in her comment about the book. What else did you catch that I missed?"

Colin blinked rapidly. "I'm not ... sure. Go through it line by line again?"

"I asked if I was better off keeping or breaking my deal with Suit. She said if I keep the deal I must find death – only she made it sound capitalized – and if I didn't, then death would find me first."

"Well," said Nariko, "you've already had two attempts on your life today, which is exceptional even for you."

"And the day's not over yet," said Colin.

"So it could be that Fire Eyes was going to kill you either way. Maybe offered you surrender as an attempt to get you to lower your guard."

"Maybe." Heath ran his fingers through his hair and scratched at the soft spot at the back of his head, just above the bandage. "Next I asked what opposition should concern me most, and that was when she warned me about the book, which Colin already shed some light on."

"That it's evil," said Nariko, "and may try to corrupt you."

"Maybe," said Heath, "but it also may be that the book resists being found. Or resists being found by me, since I don't want to use it. Or maybe it doesn't want to go to my landlord. Either way, the book itself might throw obstacles at us."

"That hardly seems fair," said Colin. "If this book turns out to be some kind of mastermind—"

"Let's deal with that if we have to," said Heath, glancing at his coal to see that it had a decent burn going. A good hour left to it, which would be more than enough for his purposes. "When I asked about the best way to survive, she said that my only future lies in my past."

"That's not how you said it earlier," said Nariko. Colin nodded.

Heath closed his eyes and jogged his memory. "No, she said my only future lies *through* my past. You guys think there's a difference?"

"Sounds like you have to confront something from your past," said Colin. "Overcome something you failed last time. Vizinha maybe. Or maybe—"

"When did you last hear from your uncle?" said Nariko.

Heath felt every line in his face smooth and that old, cold fear spider-climbing its way up his spine.

Uncle Andre.

The very last person on earth Heath wanted to see again.

COLD EARTH ON A HOT NIGHT. LOOSE DIRT, CRUMBLY. RECENTLY DUG out for a shallow grave. A grave where thirteen-year-old Heath lay half covered with shovelfuls of topsoil. Shaking in nothing but his tighty-whiteys. Shivering. Pleading with his uncle.

"I'm sorry, Uncle Andre! I didn't mean to!"

Metal scraping sound of a shovel picking up dirt. Hesitation.

"Didn't mean to what, boy?"

No idea. Heath was only guessing that he'd done something wrong. Still, there had to be a right answer here. Like this was just the most extreme of those weird tests his uncle had been giving him all month out here on the farm. Tests that had Heath seeing things he'd never seen before. Hearing things that most people would never know were there.

But if there was a right answer, Heath couldn't imagine what it was.

Didn't help that he couldn't quite think straight. His head felt stuffed with cotton that smelled like cedar and ginseng and licorice and red pepper. Like the smoke Uncle Andre "bathed" Heath with ... earlier. How long ago was that?

Heath's limbs didn't work right after the "bath." Dropped him straight on the floor of the bathroom.

The next thing Heath knew, he was here in the shallow grave.

Another shovelful of dirt landed on his belly.

"I was weak!" Heath guessed. "I wasn't strong enough for the bath. But I will be. I swear to you."

Uncle Andre hesitated with another load of topsoil ready to drop. Humor in his voice when he said, "Swear to who, boy?"

"Swear to God. To Jesus on His cross."

Uncle Andre's chuckle. Low down, like it all happened in his belly and some just happened to escape his mouth. A sound so much like Dad's own laugh it turned Heath's stomach.

"Wrong answer, boy." More dirt. "Not a test, anyway. Done with tests, you and me, and you know why."

More dirt.

Heath tried to think, but his thoughts poured like molasses. Molasses, poured on bread to offer Papa Ghede or maybe the Baron. Just the thought of the Baron was enough to make Heath's teeth chatter. The Baron was scary. Too scary for Heath.

That was it!

When Uncle Andre took Heath to those crossroads the night before, Heath had...

Heath had screamed and cried until Uncle Andre brought him home.

Heath opened his mouth to give his answer. To hope it really was just a test and not something worse. Heath had seen just enough to have an inkling of how bad "worse" could get.

Uncle Andre started speaking, so Heath held his tongue. But Uncle Andre wasn't saying English words. It was the kind of talk he did with Dad sometimes, something they knew from their youth, and it always made Grandma tell them to stop.

But Heath could pick out one word from what Uncle Andre was saying as he kept shoveling dirt. Baron. Only he didn't pronounce it like Heath did. Uncle Andre said it like it was the last two words in the question, "What did the bear own?" all smushed together.

"Right you are, boy," said a voice *right next to Heath*. High and soft, whispery and thin, like from the mouth of an old man who had all the time in the world to say what he wanted to say.

Heath screamed so loud and sharp it tore at his throat. A scream that went on until Uncle Andre shut him up with a face full of dirt that went straight into Heath's mouth and made him sputter and choke while his uncle laughed.

"Don't call your uncle's attention to me, boy, or I can't do you much good."

Heath couldn't have spoken right then anyway. He was too busy coughing and spitting, though he could hear every word the spirit was saying. And Heath knew it was a spirit. Two things Heath had learned for sure this month out on his uncle's farm. Spirits were real, and so was magic.

"Your uncle means to offer you up to the Baron just like a Christmas present. You'd be just the kind of present the Baron likes, too. Innocent, but not too innocent. Aware of magic, but not a clue what it means or how to use it."

Heath could feel his face turning blue. One chunk of dirt had lodged just wrong at the back of his throat, and since he couldn't move so much as his neck, all he could do was try to cough it free. But so far nothing worked. His belly started jerking. His lungs started crying. His eyes started spitting out tears like drizzle making way for the storm.

Panic did cut away some of the cotton in Heath's head though. Helped make the fear that much sharper.

But then the clog was gone. Just as fast as that, sweet, sweet air started flowing down Heath's throat again.

"There," said the spirit. "That's better. Now maybe you can pay some attention when I'm talking to you."

Heath nodded. His poor throat wasn't ready to even rasp out a yes.

"Now your uncle, he's going to get something mighty fine from the Baron for an offering like what you got inside you. And since you were just a little fool who put yourself in his hands, he's got the proper right to do it with or without your say. You understand what I'm telling you, boy?"

"Ye—" the rest of the word wouldn't come out, but the spirit kept talking all the same.

"Save that poor throat of yours. If you're smart, you're going to need it in a moment." Over the sounds of Uncle Andre shoveling more dirt, Heath would have sworn he heard piece of wood tap against a stone. "Now, boy, it's nothing to me if your uncle and the Baron have some kind of agreement. The Baron's good at contracts, maybe better than I am. Still, you got something in you, boy. Got enough curiosity to get you killed, and enough spirit to let you survive all the same."

Heath desperately wanted the spirit to get to the point. His legs were all covered now, and Uncle Andre's voice got louder as he kept a steady rhythm of shovelfuls of dirt coming down onto Heath's pelvis.

"So, I say to myself, I see here before me just the kind of boy I like to work with. And I know I'm not the only one. So, I'm here to offer you a deal, boy. You say to me, 'Papa Legba, help this young fool,' and I'll stand between you and the Baron tonight. And your uncle, he'll know why."

"Papa—"

"Not just yet," said Papa Legba with a bubbly little chuckle. "You gotta let me finish first. Good to see you're eager though. So, I'm giving you a choice of help. If you want, I can put that clog of dirt back in your throat and let you die right quick before your uncle makes his deal. You'll be dead, but Brigitte will have your bones and Ghede will take your angel back across the water where you belong."

Heath started whimpering.

"Or, I can save your life too, but if I'm going to go to that much trouble, you've got to promise to work with me. Not just so you understand how to offer me a proper thank-you for all I'd be doing, but so you learn a thing or two and maybe figure out how to put your uncle in his place your own self."

In Heath's youthful ignorance, that sounded like no choice at all.

"Papa Legba," he rasped, "please save this young fool so I can work with you and learn all about hoodoo."

No sooner were the words out of Heath's mouth than his head cleared. And he could move his arms and legs. But the best part was what Heath heard.

"What?" cried Uncle Andre. "No! Ba*ron*, where are you going? What..."

Heath could see his uncle looking down at him now. Work boots and overalls. Face as dark as Dad's, only with a chin a little less prominent and the kind of anger in his dark eyes that Heath had never seen in his father's.

"Oh. Oh ho ho." Now Uncle Andre was grinning that bright grin under the full moon's light. "Boy, you just fucked up something important for me. And damn you if you don't know it, lying there smelling like Papa Legba's pipe. Well, all right, boy. You and me, we're kin after all."

Uncle Andre leaned down and offered the shivering and very confused Heath a hand up. But before Heath could take another step, or even free his hand, Uncle Andre pulled him in close.

"But, nephew, I only got one more shot at what you fucked up for me tonight. So if it don't work, you better believe I'm going to send something to your window one night. Something that will let you know just how happy I am about the way you paid me back for my hospitality."

Heath could only chatter and shiver, both from cold and from the look in his Uncle's eye. But he could also smell the faintest strains of sweet tobacco smoke.

"And don't you forget, boy. You may learn a thing or two, but I'll always know more."

"I might not be evil enough to use the *Black Book*," said Heath with a shiver, "but it would be just my uncle's brand of bourbon."

He wasn't on his uncle's farm now, and he wasn't thirteen. Heath was a full-grown man. And he wasn't all alone. He was standing in the fancy kitchen of one ally while another gave him the kind of worried look she used to when they were dating and the subject of his uncle came up.

"We don't know he's involved," said Nariko, sliding off the white marble counter and stepping close so she could put a hand on Heath's shoulder.

"Why have I never heard of this uncle before?" asked Colin, handing Heath a Teufelsbrau IPA.

Heath drained the beer and burped before he answered.

"I don't talk about him much. What do you say about a blood relative who tried to offer you to Baron Samedi for the power to make zombies?"

"*Zombies?*" asked Colin. "Why would anyone want to make brain-eating—"

"Not movie zombies." Heath shook his head and flared his nose in a deep breath to try to slow his heartbeat. "Real zombies. The kind who work his farm now in New York. The kind he can send into your dreams."

Heath crossed himself and muttered a brief prayer to Papa Ghede.

"Anyway, he's tried to kill me three times since then, but I'm not sure how serious any of the attempts were. Could have been tests, like the ones he gave me that summer on the farm. He could be trying to figure out how far I've come in my power since he last saw me."

"Or maybe he gave it his all," said Nariko, taking Heath's empty bottle and setting it with the growing collection beside the brushed-steel sink. "Maybe that's why he hasn't tried in a few years. He knows he can't get you."

Heath smirked. "Now who's being dumb in all the wrong ways?"

Nariko smiled back, but Colin cleared his throat.

"All right, so your uncle may be in the game too. That doesn't change anything. We still have to get the book first, so ... wait. Zombies. Even the kind of zombies you're talking about are still a death thing, right?"

"Yep. Body dies but then rises again, obedient to my uncle, who has the spirit trapped in a jar. Both the flesh and the spirit serve him." Heath pushed out another slow sigh, but it wasn't helping with his heart rate. "This is *Vodou* stuff, not hoodoo. Never heard of a rootworker making zombies. He must be a *bokor* now—"

"The point is," said Colin, "you have to find Death before Death finds you."

"If you're suggesting I cut a deal with the Baron..."

"I know you've worked with him before." Nariko's words were hushed, like she was giving away one of Heath's secrets. Almost reverent enough to make him laugh.

"Little things. Some of the best curses I know I learned from the Baron. But nothing that would require a serious bargain, and nothing involving zombies."

"You know," said Colin, slowly, like he was afraid of the response he'd get. "If you want to find a gentler path, I could lend you a couple of books. *Swami Force* maybe, or *Voltarr Power*. Get you some magic that doesn't involve—"

"It's all the same, man." Heath shook his head, but then looked up at Colin's worried expression and snorted. "You sit there and tell yourself it's not, but you're lying. And deep down, you know it."

Nariko grabbed three more beers from the fridge. Behind Heath he could smell the charcoal burning in his censer. But he watched Colin shake his head, almost with pity.

"We don't all live in the same dark world you do, Heath."

"Really?" Heath grinned, and told himself that that grin looked nothing like his uncle's. "Well, we have a couple of hours before midnight. While I get some work done here, why don't you leave your amulets on the kitchen table, strip off your protection spells, and take a little walk from, say, Pioneer Park down to the river. I don't care which street you take."

"That doesn't mean—"

"No." Heath straightened up and stepped close to Colin. "You really think your world's so bright and shiny? You take that walk and see what happens."

Colin looked down at his cherry hardwood floor, not daring to deny what they both knew. Magic gave a person power, but it made that person a dozen times more appealing to the *things* that stalked the night. Without his protections, Colin wouldn't make it three blocks before something made a meal of him. Or worse.

Colin finally mumbled a refusal and accepted a beer from Nariko. Nariko gave Heath a quit-it look as she shoved a cold, sweating beer against his chest.

"I..." Heath puffed out a sigh that left his shoulders hanging forward. "I'm sorry, Colin. I know you were only trying to help, and I know your books are big on positive spin. But I know too damned much to smile and pretend the world's a happy place."

"So you see why *he's* fun to bring to parties," said Nariko. "How about we toast to light in the darkness?"

Colin wrinkled his brow, then it seemed to Heath that a smile dragged itself onto Colin's face, with humor on its heels, despite whatever Colin's plans might have been.

Colin raised his beer. "To light in the darkness."

"To light in the darkness," said Heath with an exasperated smile, "and we little fools who carry it."

All three drank, and this time Heath managed to appreciate the smooth flavor of the IPA.

"Anyone have any other brilliant ideas about the Sybil's cryptic utterings?"

Nariko and Colin looked at each other. Colin shook his head. Nariko shrugged and drank another swig of beer.

"Right then," said Heath. "How about I get to some spell work before I have to light another coal?"

"Wait," said Colin. "Did your landlord give you any idea where he expected you to find the *Black Book*, and how you might recover it?"

"Wouldn't have taken the job if he hadn't," said Heath, digging through his backpack for candles and a pale green felt poppet. "But that's an issue for tomorrow."

Heath straightened up and gave his friends a smile that wasn't his father's, or his uncle's, or even his mother's. It was all his, a little high on the left side, a hint of a wink to his right eye, and a real sense of pleasure from within.

"Right now, it's time for me to introduce that karcist bitch to some down home gris-gris."

5

—————

A WHITE MARBLE KITCHEN ISLAND WITH PINK AND BLUE SWIRLS FELT like a downright surreal place for Heath to light candles, burn incense, and cast spells. The whole airy kitchen felt wrong for his kind of work, surrounded by white oak cabinets and brushed-steel appliances and hardwood floor. His own work space smelled like old herbs and camphor, and it had herbs hanging from the ceiling to dry, handmade candles everywhere — a proper rootworker's habitat.

Casting in Colin's kitchen felt like he'd been hired by Martha Stewart to hex Oprah on a shoot for *Better Homes and Gardens*.

The thought made Heath chuckle, especially after his tense moment with Colin, and he heard Nariko and Colin shift back and forth where they stood behind him with their Teufelsbrau IPAs. Curious, but unwilling to interrupt Heath to ask.

He'd tell them later. If he remembered. But first, he had two bits of work to do.

Two piles of red-brown hair in front of the censer. The bigger pile he slid to the side, next to the pale green felt poppet, a fine-point black marker, three strands of Devil's Shoestring, a packet of red chili powder, and a few other things he'd need later.

It was the smaller pile that mattered first. No point in reaching out for poppet work when Salt Bitch – so nicknamed because she'd drawn a sigil in salt back at Foxy – had to have defenses in place. Heath even had some idea of what kind.

All those western ceremonialists – karcists, as some of them called themselves – made a twice-daily-or-more habit of their banishing rituals, which Heath thought was ridiculous. Cleansing and banishing were like bleaching a cutting board. A good idea every once in a while, but do it too often and the meat starts tasting funny.

And most of them didn't stop there. Most of them finished those too-frequent banishings with extra protective spells, and maybe shoved more magic into an amulet or two, engraved in some precious metal or other.

No, Heath couldn't count on being able to reach out and smack Salt Bitch like she was just some hapless banking executive. But there were ways of slipping in past defenses, for those who had a little subtlety and patience.

So Heath laid out other herbs and frosted glass vials and three powdery incenses he was considering. Truth was, so much of hoodoo, for Heath, came down to knowing how to work with what he had, rather than following the kinds of recipes found in musty old tomes. Or even musty relatively recent tomes, like the ones Colin used.

Finally he pulled the cork out of a vinegar-filled blue-glass bottle that he could hide in his hand, and set the bottle and cork right next to the censer where he could grab them quickly. Next to them he placed a narrow strip of red ten bark, and a piece of scarlet string.

Heath picked up a tiny stem of orange wanderwood and twisted it around the smaller pile of hair, and as he did he mumbled to it. "Some pants fit like a second skin and you don't know they're there. Good shirt'll be like that too. Little wanderwood, you just wrap that hair up tight, and you wrap Salt Bitch up with it like a second skin. You do that for me."

Once the wanderwood was coiled tight, Heath held up his first backup vial of holy water. He poured a drop on the hair. "One body." He poured another drop. "One mind." A third drop. "One soul."

Next he tipped a drop of Church Oil onto his thumb, and

anointed the hair as he said, "With water I baptize you, and with oil I anoint you. Salt Bitch is your name."

He did that twice more.

Three dried pine needles went onto the coal next, just enough juice left in them to let out an echo of their scent as they burned. Then a single finger-like leaf of silverweed, adding a tang to the faint smell of pine. Finally he dropped in asafetida, a leaf so rank that Heath could hear Nariko and Colin quick-step to the corners of the kitchen as the odor reached them.

Heath held the hair and wanderwood in the gray smoke, turning them left and right so every little bit got bathed in the fumes.

"Seep and bank," cooed Heath to the hair. "Seep and bank, Salt Bitch. Ease in like a mist they do. Nothing to see as they come. Nothing to hear. Nothing to smell. Nothing to feel. Nothing to taste. They follow the wanderwood, and the wanderwood is part of you now. Twined in and mixed up and all the same. Seeping right into you they come, and what they carry you can't resist."

Heath smiled. "But don't you fret none, Salt Bitch. These little herbs can't hurt you. Too small. Too minor. Not so much as a buzz or a chirp. Won't even touch you. They'll stick along the wanderwood, yes they will. They'll stick along the wanderwood and coat you thick and tight. Cozy they are, like sweet warm spring air after a cold tax assessor's office."

Heath licked a pennyroyal leaf, savored the acrid-mint taste, and wrapped that leaf around the hair and wanderwood. "And here are your shields." Another. "Your armor." Another. "Your defenses." Another, and now the hair and twisted stick were entirely surrounded by pennyroyal. "All the little magics you put between you and the world around you to keep you safe."

Heath took his thumbnail and scratched a pentacle onto one leaf. He put a drop of Abramelin Oil on his thumb and rubbed it into the pentacle.

"Sealed by Solomon himself, just like all those old books tell you to do."

Heath pinched the tiny, barely visible tip of the wanderwood and held the bundle over the smoke again. He tapped the pennyroyal leaves free so they fell onto the coal. The leaves were green still, and started smoldering before they would ever catch fire, though the oil helped.

But Heath wasn't watching. He was already tying the hair and wanderwood to the red ten bark with the piece of scarlet string. His fingers whirled as they wound it tight and finished with a quick knot. He shoved the bundle down into the little vinegar bottle and slapped its cork back into place.

"Right," he said aloud to himself. "Defenses burning away and the moment they're gone" – Heath pointed to the blue-glass bottle – "she'll be just befuddled enough that she won't get them back in place before I finish Phase Two."

"It's like watching an evil Iron Chef," said Colin.

"Hush!" said Nariko. "It's puppet time!"

Heath gave her a cockeyed grin and wiggled his eyebrows.

Heath was glad of the taste of the Teufelsbrau India Pale Ale on his tongue, and even of the slight buzz the two strong beers had given him. Made the roadside dung odor of the asafetida – only slightly moderated by the acrid mint of the burning pennyroyal – more tolerable.

He hoped Colin wouldn't have trouble getting the stink out of his beautiful kitchen. Though Heath had to admit that a tiny part of him felt good at giving the photo-quality décor a lived-in touch, even if in smell and not in appearance. Heath suspected that Nariko – hiding from that smell over in one corner of the kitchen – knew this about him. That perverse tendency was probably part of the reason she liked to have him over to her parents' house.

Heath took a step to his left, where the pale green felt poppet lay awaiting its fate on a swirl of pink and blue in the white marble of the kitchen island. Heath sewed all his own poppets by hand, and this one was the length of that hand, a little over seven inches. With no distinguishing characteristics, the poppet could serve equally well for a male or female target, depending on his needs at the time.

Next to the poppet he had already laid out some of what he expected to need. A fine-point black marker, three strands of Devil's shoestring, a packet of red chili powder, and a pile of herb packets he could dig through as needed.

The marker was first. He wrote "Salt Bitch" on the front, and underneath that he added, "Property of Heath Cyr." He flipped the doll over and pulled down a short, black zipper sewn into the back.

Heath picked up the three pieces of Devil's shoestring. He smacked them five times on his own left wrist, then held them up before his face and fanned them out. "Little of my own pain to wake you up, Devil's shoestring. You and me, we've got work to do and a score to settle, and I think we can do both at the same time." He smacked the three strands five times on his other wrist. Then he smacked the poppet on the head and belly, five times each, in an alternating pattern.

He slipped the Devil's shoestring inside the poppet.

Heath picked up the packet of chili powder next and addressed its spirit as he had the Devil's shoestring's.

"You and me, we know each other already, chili powder. And you know the kind of work I ask you to do. And this Salt Bitch, I guaran-damn-tee you she's got it coming. Tried to kill me *and* my friends, and messed up a good restaurant in the process."

Heath put five pinches of chili powder inside the poppet.

A single shaving of cedar wood went in next, with Heath telling it how Salt Bitch threw fire without worrying what she burned. Then three bits of licorice root, activated by some of Heath's own saliva. And finally three pinches of rich, whiskey-soaked tobacco, prayed over in the name of Papa Legba.

Heath zipped up the doll, then baptized it with holy water and anointed it with church oil, naming it Salt Bitch, and this he did nine times.

Heath had some good, fine pins waiting in his backpack, not to mention a knife. And he had a burning coal not much more than a foot and a half from him. He had all kinds of ways he could hurt Salt Bitch for what she did.

But that was what his uncle would have done, and his uncle was still a fresh thought in Heath's mind. Uncle Andre would have used that poppet for something truly nasty. Maybe even nastier than Heath could imagine, and he could imagine quite a bit.

Heath could have done a bunch of those things too. If he didn't mind the risk of turning into his uncle.

Instead Heath held that poppet up in both hands and addressed all the saints and gods and anyone else who might be listening in.

"Papa Legba, hear me. Papa Legba, hear this words of this little fool. Papa Legba, carry my words to all the Lwa, and if you judge my words worthy, carry them all the way to the Highest High."

Heath bowed his head and drew a slow breath.

"By the love that Jesus Christ bears for all us little sinners, I swear that this woman I call Salt Bitch tried to kill me and my friends today. She asked me to not do something I promised to do – something that she gave me no reason to believe would hurt her or hers – and when I refused her she gave killing me her best shot."

Heath drew the sign of the cross three times.

"By the words of the man who taught me, I have the right to kill her. By the deeds I have seen my peers perform, I have the right to kill her. By the need to preserve my own life, I have the right to kill her. But I do not want to kill her. So I see only one way out."

Heath dug into his backpack for purple string and pulled out a spool the size of his fist of royal purple eighth-inch cord. He set down the poppet and held up the spool. He drew the sign of the cross over it, then a pentacle, then another cross.

"*In nomine patri, et fili, et esiritu sancti.*"

Heath began to coil purple cord around the poppet.

"In the name of Jesus Christ, I bind your power. Magic will not answer your call. In the name of Jesus Christ I bind your power. Angels will not answer your call. In the name of Jesus Christ I bind your power. Spirits of this earth will not answer your call. In the name of Jesus Christ I bind your power. Demons will not answer your call. In the name of Jesus Christ I bind your power. Familiars will not answer your call."

Over and over Heath repeated those words as he wrapped the poppet in purple cord. Until at last it was entirely enveloped. Only then did he finally cut that cord, and knot it, saying, "One way out. Make amends for what you did today. Make amends to me, to my friends, to your vessel, to your vessel's lover, and to the restaurant. Only then, if God and the Lwa see fit, may your magic return."

"Oh, come *on*," said Nariko from her corner of the kitchen, the dark glass bottle of her current beer gripped tightly in her fist. "All that work for a little binding?"

"Didn't sound so little to me," said Colin, from the opposite corner. He was dangling his beer by the neck. "Lotta conditions for getting her magic back."

Heath said nothing as he grabbed his third Teufelsbrau IPA from the fridge. This would be his last of the night, despite the half-case still chilling in Colin's well-stocked fridge. He popped the top and took a long pull, forcing himself to focus on the taste of the beer, the wet chill of the bottle in his hand.

Anything but the spells he just cast. Even a momentary mental distance helped seal them off.

Besides, Heath had always found beer good for grounding himself in the mundane after working magic.

"She has information we may need," said Nariko. "It would have been nice if you at least compelled her to help us."

"He did better than compel," said Colin. "Any help she gives us has to be willing."

"Anytime you two are finished backseat casting, let me know."

Heath stepped back up to the marble island and dropped the lid back on the bedpan, sealing off the smoke and giving them all a rest from the rank odor of burning asafetida in the censer. He set down his beer and started cleaning up by shoveling herb packets back into his backpack.

"You're not your uncle," said Nariko, in the same firm tone she'd said the same words at least a dozen times before. But what followed was different, at least. "Compulsion for defense is hardly the same thing he'd do."

"That's not why." He paused with his sigil-covered incense box in his hand. "She was stupid and clumsy. Hired help, at best, trying to make a name for herself with a big show."

Heath leaned back against the counter and folded his arms, incense box still in one hand.

"The vessel she used, that guy's going to need years of therapy. His lover too. Their relationship might not survive it. Salt Bitch probably hurt even more people physically, with smoke inhalation if not fire. And Foxy is losing money every hour it's closed, on top of whatever damage she did. Who knows if they can even afford to re-open."

Heath smacked his incense box against one palm.

"That's a whole lot of lives and livelihoods messed up because she was stupid and clumsy. She's got no business using magic. Maybe if she figures out how to make reparations to those she harmed, maybe then she'll develop some sense of responsibility."

"Noble," said Nariko, "but in the meantime anything she *does* know is lost to us."

Heath tucked his incense box down into his backpack.

"Maybe not," said Colin. "I might be able to use my pendulum to figure out which hospital the ambulance took her to."

"A map would work just as fast for that," said Heath, organizing his herbs. "We were either closer to OHSU or Legacy, and the ambulance will go to the closer one. She might be out by now anyway."

"Fine," said Colin. "Use logic. Then I shall summon the mighty powers of my laptop to see what mysteries they can reveal to us."

Colin turned and left the kitchen, and the moment Heath heard Colin's shoes reach the carpet, Nariko stepped in close.

"I'm not saying you're wrong," she said, barely loud enough for

Heath to hear over the sounds of Colin setting up his computer in the dining room. "But you could have used her as a link to find the people who hired her. Even if she knew nothing, you could have used her to learn things we need to know."

Heath bit the inside of his cheek to hold back the words, "That's what your mother would have done." Which just went to show that he had learned *something* since they broke up.

"There are enough people after this book that it may not matter," he said. "And besides, by morning we'll figure out who she is, and from there it's a short step to who she's working for. And don't forget, she does owe us now, if she ever wants to cast another spell."

Heath smiled, and somewhere inside those jade eyes of hers, Nariko looked like she wanted to smile back. But that smile had no real chance of reaching her lips. Not when she had a point to make.

"This time," she said, louder now to match Heath, but both of them still quiet. "This route may have worked for us this time, but before this business is all said and done, it's going to get ugly. And I think you know that. Tell me you're ready to do what needs doing, or I'm out."

Nariko quirked her lips in an echo of Heath's own smile, but her eyes were serious.

"I still say you're too pretty to be a corpse. But I won't watch you kill yourself trying to be noble."

"I'll do what needs doing," said Heath, an icy sensation building in his gut as he said the words. "But if – all right, *when* – this gets ugly, it won't be because I dragged it into the gutter."

"Good enough," she said, and they clinked beer bottles and drained the contents.

Colin came back into the room and Heath said, "What's the good news?"

"The good news," said Colin in a flat tone, "is that she won't be troubling anyone else with her magic. Her name was Brenda Killingworth, and according to the latest news report, she just died en route back to the hospital." Colin made air quotes as he added, "Heart failure."

Heath found himself thinking that a fourth beer might not be such a bad idea after all.

6

———

"THREE OF MY HELPERS WERE EATEN LAST NIGHT."

Weird words to hear over rich morning coffee, especially when the speaker, Colin, was wrapped up in a blue fuzzy bathrobe that looked bigger than he was.

The whole scene felt surreal to Heath. Rain pounding down outside like it was February instead of July. The three of them sitting at the white oak table in Colin's elegant breakfast nook, each in a Colin-supplied bathrobe while Heath's and Nariko's clothes tumbled together in the dryer. Nariko's robe looked as though it had been sewn out of a silk Welsh flag, complete with big red dragon on the back, while Heath's was all black flannel, except for a Batman symbol over the heart.

Breakfast enchiladas heated in the microwave, a much better smell than last night's asafetida.

It would have made for a homey scene – or the strangest morning-after of Heath's life – if Colin weren't talking about how his home-brewed spirit aides had been destroyed while out searching for information.

"Does that ever just happen?" asked Nariko.

"Never. And these had a little extra oomph of unobtrusiveness. But they got spotted and shredded like a heckler at a drag show."

"All right," said Heath, deciding that the bad news merited a little more artificial sweetener in his coffee, "let's talk about what we *do* know. My landlord said the *Black Book* is supposed to have been spotted in six different cities in the past week: New York, Chicago, Saint Louis, Los Angeles, Seattle, and Portland."

Nariko hummed the tune of *One of These Things Is Not Like the Other*, and Colin snickered.

"That's right," said Heath. "One of them has the actual *Black Book of Saint Cyprian* moving through it, and the others all have decoys."

"Why believe it's here?" asked Colin.

Heath dug his wallet out of the front pocket of his robe, opened the cracked black leather, and pulled out a strip of fabric. The main part of it was a royal red, and soft gold fringe ran all the way around the perimeter. Woven through the main body was more gold thread, in the shape of a heptagram, surrounded by tiny Hebrew and Arabic letters.

The strip of fabric was no more than two inches wide and four inches long.

Heath spread it flat on the table while the others looked closer.

"According to my landlord, this was the bookmark of Saint Cyprian."

"The bookmark," said Nariko, as though repeating the punchline of a bad pun.

"Bookmark?" Colin sounded just as puzzled, but had the decency to not sound amused about it. "I thought those old books had narrow strips of fabric woven into the binding to mark your place. Like some bibles still do."

"Apparently old grimoires are the exception," said Heath with a half-shrug. "Anyway, my landlord said that the first team he sent after the book failed to gain it, but got away with the bookmark—"

"Whoa whoa whoa," said Nariko, hands up for an all-stop. "*First* team? You have five seconds to explain."

"Apparently Suit has lots of money and lots of people, but none of them with a scrap of magic. He sent a group to purchase or otherwise acquire the grimoire—"

"Otherwise acquire?" asked Colin.

"Only half the team came back, and this is what they recovered."

"So you took this job," said Nariko, "knowing that your landlord is a gangster willing to kill for what he wants. And you still want to give him a big nasty book of black magic?"

"He's a businessman, not a gangster."

Nariko let her fluttering eyelashes and smirk say her words for her. *Dumb in all the wrong ways.*

"I have to say," said Colin, slowly, "I'm not sure I can go along with this. I mean, I don't mind risking my life to help you out, but this sounds like offering a fleet of drones to the Mafia."

"Two things, if I may," said Heath, folding his hands on the table and sitting up straight as though at a negotiating table, not a kitchen table. "First, anyone who wants this book has something bad in mind for it. If we get our hands on the book first, we may be able to do something about that."

"Which would explain why the book itself might try to avoid us," said Colin.

"Second," said Heath, even louder, "there's something odd about all this."

"Something?" said Nariko, her sculpted eyebrows high.

"Suit offered me the deal because, in his own words, he knew I wouldn't want the book for myself."

Heath rolled his lips around, trying to figure out how to explain to them an itch he'd been trying to scratch since he agreed to the bargain.

"No one's offering to sell the book. But whoever has it can't be using it, or at least not seriously. Otherwise he ... or she ... would have shown up to reclaim the bookmark, probably with a host of demons riding shotgun."

"So why do they want it?" said Nariko.

"I'm not sure anyone *has* it."

Colin and Nariko glanced at each other, but Colin spoke first. "Come again?"

"You guys know about the homing spell I have on my backpack. If it's separated from me and I need it, the backpack will find its way to me."

"I always thought that was neat," said Colin.

"Are you saying that the grimoire *escaped*?" said Nariko. "On its own?"

"Why not?" Heath sipped from his cooling coffee. Almost too sweet now, but still good. "This thing's some kind of holy relic, right? Or unholy relic anyway. So maybe it was held by the Vatican and something slipped in the safeguards. The book got out."

"Then the book must be going somewhere." Nariko frowned and fiddled with the handle of her coffee cup. "Or to someone."

"Maybe not," said Heath. "Maybe it sort of ... wanders, while waiting for someone it deems worthy to come for it."

"Why give up the bookmark?" asked Colin, his own cup of coffee seemingly forgotten in his hands.

"Test maybe. Suit believes the bookmark can be used to track the grimoire, and from the little time I spent checking it out that night, I think he's right."

"What happened to the rest of the first team?" asked Nariko. "Why didn't we hear about it on the news?"

"Didn't make the news. It was a farmstead in Hillsboro. Details are sketchy, but three members of the team died. The rest ... quit his employ."

"So the book killed half the team and your landlord killed the rest of them," said Nariko. "Charming fellow."

"I don't know that." Heath focused on his coffee so he didn't have to see her expression.

"And tracking spells people are using to find the book," said Colin, "may be finding the bookmark instead."

"Would explain how some people are finding us," said Heath, still looking into cup. "Contagion's a bitch."

"So let me get this straight," said Nariko. "Your whole plan is to get the book, then figure out what to do with it?"

"Maybe it can be de-fanged."

"The cracks of Mount Saint Helen's doesn't have the right *ring* to it," said Colin.

Nariko punched him on the shoulder, hard enough to merit an exaggerated "Ow."

"My landlord could never hold onto this thing anyway. He doesn't know anything about magic. Or maybe he knows enough to talk shit at Croatoan over Pabst Blue Ribbons with the other wannabes. But no way a sentient grimoire – because that's what we're talking about whether we want to admit it or not – will settle for tutoring a toddler when it could soar with a post-doc."

"Easier to mold the toddler," said Colin. "If the thing's sentient, we don't know its motivations."

"If the stories are true," said Heath, "then Cyprian was the badass of his time, and he shoved all his dark magic into the book. It'll have plenty to teach anyone who tries to use it, and the experienced practitioner won't need to waste time on the basics."

"Fair enough," said Colin.

"But it let go of the bookmark," said Nariko.

"Yes," said Colin, eyes widening. "And now *you* have it, Heath."

Above the stove, the microwave dinged.

***

HEATH FELT ICICLES TRICKLE THEIR WAY UP HIS SPINE AND THROUGH HIS bowels. For just one moment he felt like he was thirteen again with his uncle shoveling dirt on top of him.

The bookmark lay between the three of them on Colin's kitchen table. Like a tiny, sinister tapestry of occult power. Heath could only stare at it. Was Colin right? Was Suit nothing but a conduit to help the most evil grimoire this side of the *Necronomicon* find its way to Heath?

"Colin," said Nariko, "get those breakfast enchiladas from the microwave. I'll pour us another round of coffee."

Nariko leaned in and whispered in Heath's ear, "And you pull yourself together." Then she got up, and the two of them clinked and clicked their way through preparing food and drinks, respectively.

Heath felt a mad urge to burn the bookmark on Colin's gas stove. To grab everything crucial from his apartment and start running. New Orleans, maybe. Or Haiti. Didn't he still have relatives in Haiti? Small island, hard for a book to reach him there...

Hard to hide there too. Plus, hard to earn money as a hoodoo man when he'd be surrounded by *manbos* and *houngans* and *bokors*.

No. This didn't make sense. If the grimoire was so powerful it could get Suit to spend lives chasing it and draw the attention of what seemed to be a growing number of would-be wielders, why wouldn't it just show up on Heath's doorstep? It wasn't as though Heath was in the habit of ignoring books...

...of course, anything that showed up on his doorstep might be an attack. Heath would have reacted appropriately.

But there had to be ways. If the grimoire was sentient. And if it planned to come to Heath. Heath leaned down for his backpack, but it wasn't under the table.

"Colin," said Heath, "where's my backpack?"

"In the hall closet where it ought to be when you aren't using it."

Heath stepped past his bathrobed friends to the hall closet and dug the contract out of the outer pocket of his backpack. Heath might not have been a contracts attorney, but he'd been working with spirits for most of his life. He'd learned a thing or two about making deals.

He brought the paperwork back to the kitchen table, where Colin and Nariko were already eating. Heath sipped his coffee and skimmed through the language, past the basics of the definitions, identifications, indemnities and other "standard" clauses to reach the essence of his responsibilities, on page three. He read the clause aloud.

"In exchange for the considerations listed in five (5) above, Tenant agrees to use any and all available means to locate and secure the

Property on behalf of Landlord. Tenant agrees to safeguard the Property to the best of his ability until the first available opportunity to present the Property to Landlord or Landlord's designee."

"So you have to get this thing and hold it for him," said Nariko.

"And you have to do whatever it takes," said Colin.

"No," said Heath holding up one finger, "I have to use 'any and all available means.' If this is going to stand as a legal contract, then he cannot be contracting me to do anything illegal. So illegal means are off the table."

"The point is, you have to give it to him."

"No," said Nariko, "he has to safeguard it until he has a chance to present it. Doesn't say he has to do it."

"So what?" Colin pointed at Heath with a forkful of breakfast enchilada while spiced cheddar cheese dripped onto his plate. Even Colin's breakfast enchiladas were homemade. "If you don't give him the book, you don't get apartment, money, et cetera."

"I'm not sure I see the point of worrying about the wording either," said Nariko.

"Suit's a careful, precise guy. I figured that if he wanted me to find the book, but not give him the book, there'd be a clue in the wording."

"And?" managed Colin with his mouth full.

"No idea." Heath added more sweetener to his coffee and drank a hefty slug. "He may be dealing straight or not."

"'Landlord's designee' could turn out to be you, Heath." Nariko shook her head. "If the grimoire is behind this, then Suit may not know what he intends to do either. I mean, he may think he does, but—"

"Doesn't matter," said Heath. "If Suit is playing straight, I agreed to get the book and safeguard it for a time. If not, the book will find me anyway. No matter which is true, I'll still have to deal with everyone else who wants the damned thing."

Colin snickered at the inadvertent pun, which got him a glare from Nariko.

"Especially if we're right that people trying to find the book may be finding the bookmark." Heath set his cup down. "So I guess splitting town isn't much of an option."

"I don't know," said Colin, "Heidelberg is lovely this time of year."

"Until the next Fire Eyes burns it to the ground," said Nariko. "No, I don't like the idea of giving your landlord the book, but I agree we do have to find it."

"Well," said Colin, "if your minds are made up..." Colin looked back and forth between Heath and Nariko, eyes raised with momentary hope, but no one stopped him. He sighed. "Finding things may be what I'm best at. Let me see that bookmark."

* * *

HEATH SLID THE BOOKMARK ACROSS THE KITCHEN TABLE TO COLIN. When he took his fingers away, they felt a little ... sticky. Not as though there'd been glue on the bookmark, or spilled whole cream, but as though the bookmark didn't want to let go. As though the ghost of his fingers were still touching it.

Colin reached out to touch the bookmark—

"Stop," said Heath.

Colin's hand froze in place, and Colin raised his eyes to Heath.

"Its touch ... lingers."

"Well, yeah." Colin shrugged, which looked ridiculous in the huge blue bathrobe. "That's the whole principle of association in action. The bookmark was touching the book for a long time, so bringing them together again—"

"I don't think he needs a lecture on magic theory," said Nariko. "What do you mean, Heath?"

"I feel like I'm still touching it."

"Etherically?" said Colin.

"If you like," said Heath. "Point is, this is unusual. I've touched the bookmark before and not felt this cling."

"But it's been in your possession for longer than a sunrise and sunset," said Nariko. "It's been with you on a hill and near a river. And now you try to pass it to someone else and it resists. You think it's building a link?"

"I think I need a cleansing bath, stat."

"No," said Colin. "Wait."

Heath felt the jitters all over his skin. He didn't know what bonding to the bookmark meant, but it couldn't have been good. And it might have given the *Black Book* an inroad to him.

And the last thing Heath wanted this side of facing his uncle again was to find himself under the *Black Book's* influence.

So Heath laid his hands flat on the table and focused on the feel of the flannel Batman bathrobe on his skin. The smell of the untouched breakfast burrito on his plate, and the rumble that smell gave his stomach. Normal things. Physical things.

"If we need to find the book," said Colin, "then we may need you connected to the bookmark. In fact, maybe you need to be the one casting the locator spell anyway."

"No," said Heath. "A magical act to bring the book to me sounds like a very bad idea right now."

"But we need to find the book."

"So find it," Nariko said to Colin, then turned to Heath. "I agree. Go take one of your cleansing baths."

"Look," said Colin. "I don't like this either. I wasn't kidding when I said that Heath here going over to the Dark Side is one of the worst things I can imagine. But, Heath, if you're serious about keeping a powerful relic out of evil hands, you can't afford to risk severing this connection. That might open the way for someone *else* to build a connection."

Colin put a hand on Heath's shoulder.

"This might be the only edge we have."

"Damn it," said Heath, and Nariko looked away out the window. "All right, but you guys make me a promise. If I lose myself to this grimoire, you'll kill me."

Nariko nodded once, but Colin tilted his head. "If you lose yourself to this grimoire, we might not be able to kill you."

"No transition of great power happens without a moment of

vulnerability." Nariko's voice was soft and distant, her eyes still staring at the heavy rain outside Colin's kitchen window. "As long as you fight it and don't seek it out, there'll be a moment. An eye in the storm. If that happens, I'll strike the blow."

The quiet certainty in Nariko's voice made him wonder if she had done something like this before. Years he had known this woman, but in that moment he wondered how well he knew her at all.

"Thank you," said Heath, wonder under his tone that he just thanked Nariko for promising to do something she had once joked about doing. "No cleansing bath for me, then."

"Sorry," said Colin. "You can take a second shower if you want."

"No," said Heath. "I better get started on using the bookmark to find the book."

"Eat first," said Nariko, eyes still on the horizon. "You never eat enough. In fact, Colin, would you prepare a second burrito for him?"

Colin stood and went to the freezer without a word, while Heath finally took a bite of his burrito – spicy and cheesy, with enough bacon, egg, and hash-browns to make sure his mouth knew it was eating something substantial.

The first burrito vanished in a whirl of knife and fork. At some point while he ate, Nariko turned her attention back to her own food and coffee. Colin's food seemed to just vanish without Heath never noticing him eat.

The microwave dinged to announce the second burrito's readiness.

The dryer chimed out that Heath's and Nariko's clothes were ready for a day's use.

And someone rang the front doorbell.

7

———

Heath, Nariko and Colin looked at one another across Colin's kitchen table in a moment that seemed to linger longer than the touch of the *Black Book's* bookmark.

Then the doorbell rang again.

Colin stood.

"You aren't seriously going to answer that," said Heath.

"Not everything's about you," said Colin with a half-smile. "It could just be a package delivery."

"You don't think the timing is..." started Nariko, but Colin shrugged and padded barefoot toward the front door.

Heath jumped to follow and Nariko was only a step behind them. A convoy of bathrobes and bare feet across Colin's cherry hardwood floor, still chilly in the morning's early light.

Heath didn't settle for following Colin's determined stride though. He skipped past to the window and looked out into the rain. He couldn't see the front porch from his angle, but he could see the neatly trimmed grass, and out by the curb...

"No delivery truck out there," said Heath, his fingers parting Colin's white lace curtain. "Just a black limo. Still want to answer the door?"

Colin had the decency to slow his pace and gaze out the peephole to see who stood on his porch.

"Um, Heath?" said Colin. "There's an old man on the porch who—"

"I ain't so old as all that," said a voice from the other side of the door. A voice Heath remembered all too well. "No matter what the gray hairs on my head try to tell you. Now whoever you are, boy, you open that door and let me talk to my nephew like civilized folk."

Heath's groin clutched, and his stomach puckered so hard it must have tried to hide behind his spinal cord. But he could think of nothing to say.

Not Uncle Andre. Not here.

"I'm not so sure that's a good idea," said Colin. "Maybe we could meet you downtown for lunch—"

"Boy, I have ridden in the cramped seats of two airplanes, and traveled three thousand six hundred twenty-three miles to stand here on your doorstep. Now you can either open this door, or the next time you hear my voice I won't be so pleasant and civilized as I am right now."

Nariko shook her head emphatically, but Heath sighed.

"Uncle Andre," said Heath in the strongest voice he could muster, "a civilized man does not force his company on a host who is still in his bathrobe."

"It's nearly nine a.m. By all the deals made at crossroads, boy, how late do you sleep?"

"None of us are famers, Uncle Andre." Heath could imagine the irritated flare of his Uncle's nostrils at that comment, because Heath's uncle wasn't really a farmer either. Not anymore. He hadn't done his own work in years. "Portland may not be Manhattan, but the fact is that we're still city dwellers and not used to setting up meetings before ten, at the earliest."

A tricky answer, but Heath knew Uncle Andre would taste enough truth to believe it. Heath never set an appointment before noon if he could avoid it, although Colin had eight o'clock classes two days a week, and Nariko didn't need an alarm clock to rise with the sun.

"All right then, boy, when and where for a pleasant family chat?"

Heath was tempted to name Tsarina's, but if they really were connected to the Russian mob, his uncle might be able to cut a deal with them.

"Riverfront Park near the Burnside Bridge. Eleven-thirty. Give us time to get dressed, and you to find a hotel."

"All right, boy. I'll see you then, and I look forward to meeting the two friends you have in there with you." Uncle Andre chuckled, and Heath remembered too well that low bubbling sound. "Too clever for your own good, though. Should have talked to me now when I just got into town. Give me another two hours and who knows what I'll brew up?"

"See you at eleven-thirty, Uncle."

Uncle Andre didn't say anything else, but he grinned over his shoulder at Heath from Colin's front walk. A scary image, the broad, gleaming grin from under a black umbrella.

Uncle Andre wasn't kidding about the gray hair. All his tight curls had faded from black to steel gray. He'd lost weight though, Heath could see that because the black overcoat didn't bulge. Uncle Andre moved like a bantam weight boxer in his prime instead of a man in his fifties. A light step, as though all the travel he complained about hadn't slowed him down in the least.

He'd probably already been in town for two days, or so. Probably already made some allies. Vizinha, maybe. Or that demon-conjurer, Drake. Someone who wanted bad things for Heath.

He might even have known the time and location Heath would choose for their meeting. He always seemed to be three steps ahead of Heath, ever since that night in the grave. Probably only wanted to show his face now to get Heath thinking about him. Knew Heath wouldn't open the door. And if he did, Heath would have found out *he* was the one who was unprepared.

As Uncle Andre got into the car, he grinned again and raised an index finger to his temple in a salute to Heath before closing the door.

The limo pulled away, hissing across the wet pavement.

Heath watched it go.

"You're not thirteen anymore," said Nariko. "You've come a long way."

"So has he. The last time I saw him he couldn't afford to throw money away on travel like that, much less the limo."

"A rental," said Colin from the window on the other side of the front door. "And he didn't fly first class if he felt cramped in."

"Uncle Andre would feel cramped in the only seat on a private jumbo jet. He'd say it hemmed in his spirit."

Nariko made an impatient sound.

"Look at me."

She poked Heath in the ribcage, something she hadn't done in a long time. Heath turned, but couldn't quite read the emotion in her jade eyes.

"This is your town, not his. And maybe you have enemies, but you have allies too. Real allies. People like him are always trying to out-maneuver each other. If he's been here long enough to reach out to someone like Vizinha, they're both more interested in how they can use each other than they are in striking at you."

"How did you know—"

"Because I know you." She shrugged, making the big Welsh-flag robe look somehow right on her. "Now come on. We've got two hours to prep for this, and I'm betting all three of us have tricks we want to prepare."

"After breakfast," said Colin, leading the way back to the kitchen.

"I guess I should put the bookmark back," Heath muttered, pulling out his wallet. Then he stopped right where he was standing. A dusty chill swept across his shoulders and the back of his neck.

The bookmark was already in his wallet. Not waiting for him on the kitchen table where he'd left it.

Heath shoved the wallet back in his robe pocket and forced his feet forward again before Nariko or Colin could notice.

At half an hour before noon, the rain hadn't let up. What was more, it had added plenty of lighting and thunder, to make both Ogun-Shango and Oya proud. Enough storm in July to keep most of the joggers and bikers away from scenic Riverfront Park.

But not all of them. Not here in the Pacific Northwest where it seemed that people didn't have enough sense to come in out of the rain. The most hardy, or the most dedicated, wrapped themselves in rain gear and persevered.

Still, they were few and far between enough that Heath felt confident in a certain amount of privacy.

He leaned against a pillar under the Burnside Bridge, the smell of wet asphalt and oil stronger here than the clean water scent of the Willamette. On the bridge above him a steady static of cars rushing their way across the river.

Heath stood on asphalt, not the tile of the nearby sidewalk. He'd picked a spot free of graffiti, one he was able to walk to without having to step anyplace that might be hiding goofer dust, or any of a dozen other little hexing possibilities that might pick away at his defenses.

Nothing like that would have been more than an opening salvo for Uncle Andre, but so much had happened in the last couple of days that Heath had to assume a wartime demeanor.

Trust nothing.

Past the pillar behind Heath were crisscrossing stairs that led up to the bridge, for those who wanted to walk across the river. Dangerous to have at his back, except that Nariko was watching them. She in her business outfit once more – tight jeans, form-fitting black top and bun held in place with a steel spike – leaning against the pillar opposite Heath, maybe thirty paces away. She definitely looked more deadly than Heath did in his blue-and-white striped shirt and black jeans.

Colin was around here somewhere. Invisible again, which was a trick good enough that Heath was seriously considering giving one of

Colin's books a try. If he could muddle through the over-the-top, infomercial style. *Jenny H. was living on the street and addicted to crack, but one chant later she's beautiful and healthy and courted by the richest and most handsome bachelors in Johannesburg.* Or something like that.

Maybe invisibility wasn't worth it after all.

Invisibility wouldn't have mattered for Heath right now anyway. His uncle had found him again. At Colin's house. While both Heath and Colin had spells up trying to foil trackers. Though admittedly, Heath's had probably given out around midnight. Still, none of the others after the *Black Book of Saint Cyprian* had managed to track Heath down.

But Uncle Andre did. And Uncle Andre knew that Nariko was there, through a closed door, even though she hadn't said a word.

More subtle ways to remind Heath that however much he learned, his uncle would always know more.

Just when Heath was about the check his watch again, he saw a black limousine pull up to the curb. He felt that old childhood itch to run, right behind his kneecaps. His hands felt awkward. Unsure. Maybe he should put them in his pockets. Confident. No. Maybe he should dig something out of his backpack. A little goofer dust of his own, maybe.

No. And the back of his neck felt exposed. He already had one wound there. What was he thinking, meeting Uncle Andre out here in the open? A crowded restaurant would have been better. Someplace with a bathroom window Heath could have crawled out of if things got really bad.

The door of the limousine opened, and Uncle Andre got out. Black suit, black shirt, shiny black shoes, crimson tie. Mahogany cane with an ivory handle. Uncle Andre didn't need the cane, but Heath knew why he had it.

Uncle Andre proved Heath right with every step closer. Tapping his cane at the same rhythm Papa Legba used to hide Heath the other night. Reminding Heath that Papa Legba worked with him too, maybe more than with Heath.

Uncle Andre must have seen that Heath got the message, because he grinned that same old grin. And though Uncle Andre's hair was all gray now, he didn't have any more lines on his face than he did the last time Heath saw him. The man looked positively vibrant.

"What was the third thing I taught you, boy?" asked Uncle Andre as he approached. Even with his eyes open, Heath could just about see a couple of Uncle Andre's little ghosties flitting about, checking the layout and reporting to him.

"Never show fear. It gives your enemies power."

"That's right." Uncle Andre stopped a few steps behind Nariko's pillar. She had turned her head to mark his approach, but otherwise hadn't moved. "But there you stand, stinking out fear like your black ass just saw a swastika tattoo on the cop who pulled you over."

"You still my enemy, Uncle Andre? Been a while since you sent something to my window, and your other offering to the Baron must have been good enough to do the job for you, because life seems to be treating you all right."

"The Baron and I get along just fine." Uncle Andre tapped his cane one more time before resting it in front of him under his folded hands. "And if you're willing to let bygones be bygones, then so am I. Yeah, I got a little peeved at your insolence, but you're still my kin."

"Glad to hear it," said Heath, "though I hope you don't mind my saying it's a little too soon for us to hug."

"Smart boy." Uncle Andre chuckled, then looked around. "Dramatic place for a meeting. You have any trouble getting here?"

"I didn't trip any traps you left for me, if that's what you mean." Heath tilted his head. "Leaving a present on the back gate was a nice touch."

The present was just a little annoyance. A *hot-foot charm* to keep Heath agitated when they met. Uncle Andre's grin widened, then he pursed his lips and nodded.

"Maybe you've learned a thing or two after all. Maybe even enough for me to concede that Legba was right to save you."

"Maybe?" Heath fingered the second mojo bag in his front pocket, his little extra protection for this morning.

"Maybe." Uncle Andre nodded again. "Time's gotta tell the tale on that one."

"Well," said Heath, "if you and me are burying the hatchet—"

"Not so fast, now, nephew. Things aren't even between us just yet, and I think they need to be before you and I can stop checking yesterday's footprints for nails."

Heath actually chuckled at that, and realized that his body had settled down. His gut still felt low and tight, but more like fear was a tool now than an impediment.

"Just what do you think I owe you for saving my own life?"

"A little restitution. You cost me time and power, and I think we both know there's a way you can make that right moving through this little excuse for a city."

"You can't seriously expect me to bring you the *Black Book of Saint Cyprian*."

"Cowries say you've got the best chance of getting hold of it. Even better than my own chances, and that's saying something. So you swear to me by the deal you made with Papa Legba that when you lay hands on the book, you'll give it to me as a gift, free and clear. You do that, and not only will I call things even, I'll teach you *pwen* beyond any mojo you can call."

Uncle Andre nodded his head back and forth, noncommittally.

"Maybe I'll even share the findings of the book with you. We'll see."

Heath screwed up his face tight, then let it go slack.

"I miss you, Uncle Andre. I miss the days when you were my favorite uncle, telling stories and playing ball with me." Heath shook his head. "But you're into some dark stuff, uncle. Making zombies work your lands like old plantations in Haiti."

"Zombies are good for much more than that, boy. I'll teach you that too. The Baron would love it."

"No, Uncle Andre. I won't give you that book even if I do get my hands on it."

"Maybe you're not so smart after all, boy." Uncle Andre gave his head a single slow shake and flared his nostrils in a deep sigh. "And I had such hopes for you."

He started to turn away, then stopped and turned back.

"Tell you what. You change your mind, you just leave me a note in the moonlight and one of mine will find it."

"I won't change my mind."

"You give it serious thought, nephew. I'll give you till sunrise tomorrow to reconsider. Then I'm coming for that book. And if you're in my way, well, it won't be easy consoling your father."

Uncle Andre turned and walked away, swiftly this time and with his cane tucked under his arm.

Nariko spun around the side of her pillar and whipped the steel spike from her hair, arm back and ready to throw while her hair spilled down behind her.

"Won't help," said Heath, closing the gap between him and her.

Nariko blinked and then frowned. She pointed to the six-armed spirit covering Uncle Andre's back.

"*Where did that thing come from?*"

"It's always there. One of the first real spirits I saw."

"But at Colin's house—"

"It was hiding."

Uncle Andre got back in the limo and rode off.

Nariko fixed her hair and tucked the spike back into place. She nodded.

"I'll be ready for it next time," she said.

"And I'll be ready for him," Heath said, wishing he felt as confident as he sounded.

"HE LOOKED AT ME," SAID COLIN, APPEARING BESIDE THEM UNDER THE Burnside Bridge. Nariko had to check her fist from punching, but Heath didn't move. He didn't have it in him to feel surprised right then.

Overhead a huge truck rumbled past.

"Wait," said Heath. "He *looked* at you? While you were invisible? Are you sure?"

"Positive. And it's never happened before." Colin shivered, fluttering his faded, oversized Metallica *Ride the Lightning* t-shirt. "I was behind the limo, whipping up a little spirit to keep an eye on your uncle, when he reached the passenger door. He grinned at me and said, 'You fire that thing off and one of mine will eat it.' Then he just got in the car and drove off."

"Did you send your spirit?" asked Nariko.

"I was too shocked."

Heath thought about that as he watched a man and a black lab walk past, both in slickers while the rain poured down all around. Lingering smell of garlic and hawthorn in the air, which had to have been from Uncle Andre, but Heath didn't remember smelling them in his presence.

"Do you guys smell anything?" he asked.

"Cars," said Nariko. "Oil, rain, grass from the park over there." She jerked her thumb over her shoulder. "Nothing odd."

"I ... I was just going to say wet pavement," said Colin.

"Nothing else. Nothing spicy or woody?"

"Like what?" asked Colin. Nariko only gave Heath an expectant look.

"I can smell both hawthorn and garlic."

Nariko inhaled deeply through her nose, then shook her head. Colin only shrugged.

Heath shook his head slowly. Hawthorn and garlic, together, were used for protection. But neither of his mojo bags had either, and Heath was sure he hadn't smelled them during his talk with Uncle Andre. In fact...

"Nariko, what did you smell while my uncle was here?"

"Nothing different." She tilted her head, eyebrows furrowed. "No. I didn't smell anything from him at all. Not aftershave. Not deodorant."

"Not even Florida water," muttered Heath. "How did you manage that, uncle?"

"Forgive the ignorant white boy," said Colin, "but what difference does smell make?"

Apparently Heath had some room for surprise left after all. Air rushed out his mouth, too breathy to call a chuckle, while his lips moved halfway toward a smile.

Nariko just answered the question.

"We've both known Heath long enough that we can tell by the smells when he's been working. Sometimes I can even guess the type of working from the different roots I can pick out."

Heath flashed on the way Nariko once made a game of guessing what herbs Heath had been working with as she slowly stripped him of his clothes.

"But his uncle," Nariko continued, "didn't have any of those smells. Nothing. Not even a normal kind of clean adult man smell."

"So what does that mean?" said Colin.

"It means he was hiding something." Heath shook his head. "I'm not sure how he did it, but he must have tricked the air into not carrying his scent. Which means he knew I'd learn something from it. But what? And why am I smelling herbs you two don't?"

"Now those" – said a man's voice far enough behind Heath that the speaker had to have been on the stairs – "are questions worth asking."

Heath turned while Nariko shifted so she'd be concealed from the interloper's view by the pillar beside Heath. Colin stepped behind Heath, the size difference between them enough to make the smaller man vanish.

Standing on the stairs looked like a reject from a Colonel Sanders audition. A portly white man verging on elderly, his suit as white as his short, wavy hair. A flash of gold under his left cuff implied a watch, and little round glasses on gold, wire frames made his face look larger than it probably was.

Even the man's shoes were white. Had he just come from gambling on a riverboat?

"And what do you know," asked Heath, "about which questions are worth asking?"

The man started coming down the stairs, one hand gliding down the rail rather than using it for support. A practitioner, and from the feel of him, a major player.

As the man approached, he spoke.

"Mr. Cyr, my name is Ulysses Beauregard the Third, and I have devoted my life to knowing which questions are worth asking. Not to mention deducing the most appropriate ways of asking those questions to produce the most practical answers. So I think that you will be hard pressed to find yourself a person, be that person a man, a woman, or otherwise, who is more qualified and experienced than I am at the very art of the query. So to leave the rest of that as going toward the establishment in your minds of both my identity and my *bona fides*, I shall take it upon myself to answer your question now in the most direct and concise manner possible that yet allows for the proprieties of genteel conversation."

Mr. Beauregard came to a halt beside the pillar behind which Nariko hid.

"I know a very great deal, Mr. Cyr."

"That doesn't tell me why I care."

"Very true, but in my defense you did not ask why you should care."

"Talking to you is going to be like talking to the Sybil, isn't it?"

"Not nearly so recondite, Mr. Cyr, I assure you," said Mr. Beauregard with a quiet laugh. "As proof of that and as a step toward convincing you of my good intentions, I would like to treat the three of you to lunch at the restaurant of your choosing. And perhaps as we dine we can discuss the mysteries of olfactory perception as they relate to your father's brother, and from there we might bridge the topic to our shared interest in a book recently overdue from the Vatican library."

Heath's stomach growled at the mention of lunch, and he allowed himself a slight smile.

"I know just the place."

8

———

Unlike Gripper, from the street Croatoan looked like a friendly, welcoming place. Large sign with the name in a witchy font. Smaller sign above the door reading, "Come in for a spell." Big panel windows, tinted just enough so that pedestrians in the fashionable Pearl District could admire the bustle and the animated conversations inside without actually identifying the patrons.

A private place for public conversations. A place where the occult wasn't hidden; it was open and discussed by everyone in earshot.

A place Heath, Nariko and Colin would not normally be caught dead eating a meal.

Zory, the bouncer / doorman raised his shaved eyebrows when he saw Heath approaching. Zory was two-hundred fifty pounds of tanned muscle without a single visible hair beyond his eyelashes, all packed into a sleeveless white t-shirt and tight black jeans that Heath knew were seamed to allow for high kicks. Heath knew that because he once saw Zory kick the jaw of a man tall enough to play center for the Trail Blazers without splitting his pants.

"Hey, Heath," said Zory in his high, clear voice. "Nariko. Colin." Quieter he added, "Everything okay with the wards? Maggie didn't say anything about you stopping by."

"We're here," said Nariko with a forced smile, "for lunch."

Zory blinked, then his expression cleared and his back straightened, eyes tracking someone approaching along the sidewalk. And Heath had a pretty good idea who.

"The wannabe-Colonel Sanders is treating us to lunch," he said, "if we can get a booth away from the general shouting matches."

Zory smiled and opened the door.

Heath was met by a wall of sound. Dozens of voices laughing and yelling and arguing and more all over what was either an orchestral interpretation of Celtic music or the soundtrack to one of the *Lord of the Rings* movies.

Properly speaking, Croatoan was a public house. Three big runner tables in the middle where strangers could sit together and argue interpretations of grimoires, or whatever the hell it was these people devoted endless hours to reasoning their way through. Right now it had something to do with Pluto and astrology.

Positioned around the big tables to allow free and easy access for the wait staff – women in wispy, witchy dresses and guys in tight pants and open-collared poet shirts – were nine smaller tables, all close enough to participate in the big discussions, for those with a mind to.

A little more privacy could be found along the walls. Low-backed booths that could seat six, if they were friendly. And, of course, a bar covered in occult symbols. In fact, most of the main room was covered in occult symbols, or laminated seals from grimoires, framed pictures of old woodcarvings of witches at the sabbat, magazine and newspaper stories on occult topics, and so on.

And right now every chair in sight was either filled or plainly occupied by a person standing up to make a point. Men and women in business suits alongside teenagers in lace and velvet or just black whatever (both the boys and the girls). The t-shirt-and-jeans brigade was in full force too, as were those who matched fabrics and colors to a method all their own. All body types and approaches to hygiene and makeup, from the understated to the overdone in just about every sense.

And just about every scent too. Old incenses clashed with perfumes and colognes over the pervasive fried smell of pub food.

Every one of these patrons was a student of the occult. Almost every one of them with an opinion to state loudly and often.

And Heath would have bet that not a single one of them, not even the crowd of sullen teenagers waiting for a table, had ever managed to produce a single magical effect. Heath used to waste time wondering how many of them even tried, but that was a fruitless line of reasoning. For most of them, the discussion was all that mattered. Or perhaps enough introspection and meditation to fan the spark of power within any living being.

Those were the ones in the worst danger. They had no idea what would have followed them out to their cars after a night's discussion if it weren't for Heath's repelling wards.

But right now, these innocent fools provided the perfect cover for a conversation Heath didn't want to have where anyone important could hear it.

A blonde waitress approached, pen in hand, to add them to the waiting list. Until she got a good look at Heath.

"Mr. Cyr? Do you need me to fetch the manager?"

"No thanks," – Heath glanced at her attractively positioned nametag – "Holly. I need the booth if it's free."

"Right this way," she said, over protests from the waiting teenagers about how long they'd been waiting.

Tucked away in the back corner was a booth that almost always sat empty. Maggie had once told Heath that the booth's emptiness, even when customers were waiting for tables, had generated many amusing theories from the patrons. Her favorite was that it was reserved for the spirits of the beloved dead, and that food and drinks were laid out for them every dark moon at closing time.

Heath wondered what the patrons would say if they noticed Heath and his party sitting there right now.

The point was moot. They couldn't notice. Little enchantments woven into the wood of the table and the cloth of the bench seats ensured that only the magically active could perceive people at the table. The wait staff and management had passcode enchantments in their nametags to let them hear orders and talk directly with customers seated in that booth, but even then they couldn't understand side conversations in their presence.

The booth only existed so Maggie could have a place to talk with friends when she had to mind this establishment instead of Gripper, but she allowed certain other people to use it.

Heath was one of the lucky few.

Heath and Mr. Beauregard took the inside seats, with Nariko next to Heath and Colin next to Mr. Beauregard.

"Interesting establishment," said Mr. Beauregard. "It appears to be a place of many answers and few questions, with little regard to the practical veracity of the arguments supported. I do not believe that I would be telling tales out of school if I were to suggest this is not a public house upon which you frequently bestow your patronage."

Heath drew breath to reply, but Mr. Beauregard was not finished.

"Although, given that you were properly identified by the charming young lass who escorted us to our seats, and given that this particular booth appears to be warded against the dropping of eaves, I suspect, Mr. Cyr, that you are well acquainted with the proprietor of this establishment, and furthermore that the fine protective handiwork I perceived woven into the exterior paint as well as the windows and doorframes would be yours. Are my suppositions correct?"

"Do you ever breathe?" asked Colin.

Mr. Beauregard laughed, a high sound that would have been fine to hear if it didn't remind Heath of chickens pecking at their food.

"I have been known to circulate oxygen through my system, when the mood takes me."

Mr. Beauregard winked.

Heath had been ready to laugh off Colin's question, but now he found himself wondering whether or not he'd ever noticed Mr. Beauregard breathing. He couldn't say either way, so he answered the question he'd been asked. But he also started paying closer attention.

"No, none of us usually eat here, and I'm sure you've already figured out why. And what's more I'm sure you've figured out why we're eating here now, and why this booth. So shall we—"

"Are we ready to order?" said Holly, who apparently didn't need a pad to remember her orders. Colin ordered a chili cheeseburger with chili cheese fries with "whatever Hef you have on tap." Mr. Beauregard asked for a tall glass of iced tea with a sprig of mint. Nariko declined so much as a glass of water. Heath had the haddock fish and chips with a Teufelsbrau IPA.

After the waitress left, Mr. Beauregard raised his white eyebrows at Nariko.

"When we leave today, I'll be the only one of us who can still say I've never eaten here."

Mr. Beauregard laughed again. "While I confess that I have yet to pass much time in your quaint little city, I must admit that I find fascinating the variety of deeply held beliefs and views of its citizenry. In fact—"

"With all due respect, Mr. Beauregard," said Heath, "time is pressing and we have a great deal to do."

"Yes, of course, of course." Mr. Beauregard gave Heath what he would have sworn was a chagrined bow from the neck up. "The topic, I believe, concerned a certain volume of lore that appears to be not quite so forgotten as its quaint and curious subject matter might have—"

"We might get to that topic," said Heath, "if the first one goes well. And the first topic is why I was smelling garlic and hawthorn under the bridge, but Nariko and Colin were not, and what you know about it."

"Ah, indeed," said Mr. Beauregard with a smile that gleamed with a great many small teeth, "because to understand the reason for the differentiation, we must begin by the determination of which of you were in error. Whether you, Mr. Cyr, perceived an olfactory disturbance that was not present, or whether Ms. Tachibana and Mr. Driscoll—"

"Whoa," said Colin. "How do you know my last name? I mean, Heath's practically in the phonebook, and Nariko gets all formal with people from time to time. But me? Nobody uses my last name. Not unless it's official. Heck, the last time I got *arrested* the cops all called me Colin."

"You've been arrested?" asked Nariko.

"Never charged," said Colin with a grin. "Tell you about it another time."

Mr. Beauregard looked at Colin, then at Heath. Then at Nariko, and Heath again. But apparently whatever he was hoping to see, it wasn't poker faces, which was all he got beyond the challenging look in Colin's eye.

"I do believe that I already explained the extent to which I have made a study of the questions and answers that plague us in life. In fact, I rather thought that I did a sufficiently thorough job that the matter of such mundanities as my comprehension of information freely available to the public would be taken as given."

"No one questions that you *could* find out Colin's last name," said Heath.

"The question is *why*," said Nariko.

"Well, as to that I'm afraid that I must beg your pardon," said Mr. Beauregard with a look of honest contrition. "Because our esteemed Mr. Cyr has forbidden the topic of that certain volume for the time being, and that does rather tie my conversational hands when it comes to enlightening the three of you as to precisely why I have come to your fair city of roses, why I have learned about each of you what has been necessary for me to learn, and why, as a matter of strictest fact, I came to be perambulating down that certain staircase at such a time as to bear witness to the conversation that first began our discourse not so much as half an hour ago."

"Un-fucking-believable," said Heath, eyes widening with realization at what he was seeing. Not a single breath. The mouth was moving but the words were coming from someplace else.

"What?" said Colin, but Heath already had one hand deep in his backpack for an empty blue glass bottle and the other snatching the salt and pepper shakers off the table.

"I believe that while Mr. Cyr enlightens you as to the reason for his sudden ejaculation of colloquial verbosity I shall take advantage of that time to avail myself of the facilities—"

"You're not moving," said Nariko, steel spike in hand and hair collapsing down.

"Really, I—"

Mr. Beauregard started shaking and shivering, and Heath immediately licked salt and pepper off his hand to activate it with the right intentions and spat the mixture onto Mr. Beauregard's shirt.

Mr. Beauregard shook harder, and Colin yanked out his wallet as though to use it as a mouth guard for the man, but glanced at Heath and stopped. Heath put the full weight of his own power behind his words.

"By pepper I kick you out and by salt I bind you." Heath thunked the empty bottle on the table, the cork dangling from where Heath had tied it to the neck. The blue glass displayed the variety of symbols and passages needed for the bottle to do its task. "Into the bottle, ghostie, or the Baron himself will have words with you."

All at once Mr. Beauregard stopped shaking. His head dangled forward.

"I said in and I meant it," said Heath. "Last warning or I get *rough*."

Heath watched with his spirit eyes as the ghostie trailed out of Mr. Beauregard like the vapors from a humidifier to gather inside the bottle.

Heath slammed the cork into the bottle.

"Gotcha, you little bastard," he said with a smile.

9
____

Twenty minutes later Heath, Nariko and Colin gathered once more around the marble island in Colin's kitchen with rich, sweet-smelling coffee brewing in Colin's fancy coffee maker. They had left the innocent Mr. Beauregard eating a meal at Heath's expense and convinced – thanks to a *believe-me* charm that worked very well on people who were already a little confused – that he would be fine after his fit, though he should get a check-up to be sure.

On the counter between the three of them sat the blue bottle containing the ghostie Heath had knocked out of Mr. Beauregard. Something about the scene felt ominous to Heath. Maybe it was the pouring July rain with its undertone of lightning and thunder.

"I can't believe Nariko and I both missed that possession," said Colin for the third time. But this time he followed it with, "How did you spot it, Heath?"

"Well, if it had been anything more powerful than what it is, we'd have all seen it at once. As to what tipped it, I could say it was the fili-bustering, or my uncle's choice of sending a man in all white like a Vodou *hounsi,* or even just clean living on my part. But it was your hint about the breathing."

"I was joking."

"No." Heath pointed to the bottle. "You only thought you were because the chest muscles were moving right. But the nostrils and the lips weren't flaring to match the chest, and he never paused in what he had to say. A real blowhard like that uses pauses for emphasis as well as breath."

"You're sure your uncle sent it?" said Nariko.

"Positive. I saw his ghosties flitting about while we were talking. Didn't count them though. That was a mistake. But when Colin mentioned breathing the rest came together."

"But with so many other players—"

"I'm not trying to *put this on* Uncle Andre." Heath leaned forward over the island. "It's his style, and it was a way to show me that he can send a possession so good I won't notice it until I have to. Besides. We'll know for sure when I talk to the ghostie."

"Why do you keep calling it a ghostie?" said Colin. "I'm not used to you using that word."

"'Cause I'm ninety-nine percent sure that's the *zombie astral* of one of my uncle's zombies." Heath shrugged. "Calling them by their official term makes them sound too cool."

Nariko snorted.

Heath pulled up a locally handmade ash stool and sat. He closed his physical eyes and focused on his spirit eyes. Colin and Nariko shone brightly, but Heath relaxed to their presence through a series of slow breaths. Then he dismissed them from his attention. Next he had to tune out the wards, followed by the other little spells Colin had running around the house. And there were more of those than Heath expected.

Once Heath cleared his attention of the background magic, he focused instead on the symbols and words drawn and written all over the bottle. He knew every one of them. Had drawn them by hand from memory, following all the right steps in their proper order to give those "decorations" the power to trap and hold a spirit. None of the flexibility of a proper skull candle trap, but that would have been for binding the spirit, and this little ghostie was already bound. All Heath could do was contain it and, to an extent, constrain it.

Those words and symbols glowed a bright green to Heath's spirit eyes, and they'd continue to glow so long as they continued to work.

Inside the boundaries created by the bottle, Heath could just make out a small orange wisp. It didn't quite move, but didn't quite stay still enough to form a coherent sphere. Instead it seemed to ebb and flow around itself. Like a penlight shining through a bottle of orange soda.

Was this what a person's soul looked like? Or was this what became of a soul that had been trapped and abused by someone like Uncle Andre?

"I can't free you," said Heath to the wisp. "I don't know where Uncle Andre keeps the *govi* that houses you, and even if I did it's likely a long, long way from here. But know this. I *want* to free you from service to him. If I *do* find your *govi* I'll smash it into little clay splinters and you can go on to whatever's waiting for you on the other side."

Heath nodded once, slowly.

"Taste those words, and if you find a lie in them you can tell me right now. With Damballah as my witness, if I just lied to you I'll stop talking on your honest say-so." Heath waited the length of a single breath. "So you tell me now, do you taste any lie in what I told you?"

"No." The voice was clear, and very like the clear tones that had come out of poor Mr. Beauregard while the ghostie rode him. "You have not yet lied to me."

"And by that truth I bind you. By my words I bind you. And by my heart I bind you. I can speak no lie or deception to you during this conversation, but you can speak no lie or deception to me. And by the bottle I've tied you to, you may speak only to me during this conversation, which ends when I say it does."

The ghostie flared a little brighter in agreement.

"Are you sure that's wise?" asked Nariko.

Heath ignored her.

"Was it my uncle who sent you into Mr. Beauregard?"

"It was. May I ask you questions too?"

"Answer all of my questions fully and completely and I'll allow you to ask three of your own, provided you promise not to share that information with my uncle."

"Your uncle can compel me to tell anything I know, but I can promise to mislead him about what I know to keep your secrets about those three questions."

"Fair enough." Heath shifted on the stool and straightened up. He'd bent forward again. He always did that when talking to bound spirits. "Where is my uncle staying?"

"He spent last night in the riverfront Marriott. But he planned to change hotels after seeing you. I don't know which one was next."

"How long has my uncle been in town?"

"He arrived last afternoon. But he has had servants like me in Portland for three days."

"What did he have you assigned to do in that time?"

"My job was to investigate the places of power. There were too many to cover. I focused on the parks. I—"

"That's enough on that topic for now." Heath scratched his chin. "Who does my uncle consider his three biggest competitors for the *Black Book of Saint Cyprian*?"

"You, of course. A Brazilian woman known to many as Neighbor. An Italian man called The Lammergeyer."

"Neighbor?" asked Colin as he poured coffee for the trio.

"Vizinha," said Heath, adding plenty of fake sugar to what he knew would be a strong cup. "That's what it means."

"I've heard of The Lammergeyer," said Nariko, adding cream and just a little real sugar to her coffee. "He's from Vancouver. Usually stays north of the Columbia."

"What kind of magic?"

Heath intended that question for Nariko, but Nariko and the ghostie answered it at the same time.

"I think he's a Thelemite..." started Nariko.

"Your uncle says she claims *Candomblé*, but actually practices *Quimbanda*."

"...but I'm not sure. Might be Golden Dawn, or Silver Star, or worse, maybe one of those Red Sky yahoos."

"Where is my uncle looking for the *Black Book*?"

"He skims, not hunts. His plan is to take it from whoever claims it before they master its powers."

"I don't know, guys," Heath said, turning to his friends. "If that... wait." He turned back to the spirit in the bottle. "How much will your loss inconvenience my uncle? Will it change his plans?"

"Very little, and it won't. He brought a dozen of us with him."

Heath straightened up in his chair and smiled. "Do you mean he brought your *govis*?"

"Yes. He keeps them in a satchel."

Nariko and Colin started talking in hushed, furtive tones, but Heath's focus was on the bottle. He put both hands on the cool white marble and leaned forward eagerly.

"Where is this satchel right now?"

"I last saw it in his suite in the riverfront Marriott."

"It has to be with him then," said Nariko. "If he's changing hotels it's probably in the limo."

"We could steal it," said Nariko. "While you—"

"No," said Heath. "I don't doubt how good you two are at spotting and diffusing wards, but you don't know the way my uncle thinks. I have to go along for this."

"If you are done asking questions," said the ghostie, "is it my turn?"

Heath blinked, then shrugged and sipped his coffee. Hazelnut. He'd chug this whole cup in a moment if he let himself.

"All right," said Heath, "but I may want to ask you more questions later."

"First, you have never sent a serious attack at your uncle, despite provocation. Why?"

Heath spared a glance at Nariko who, from the set of her jaw, did not like this news and would have words for him about it later.

"He's still my father's brother." Heath shrugged and drew a deep breath. "And I still love him. Not the man making zombies, the uncle I knew as a child."

"Second, what will you do with the *Black Book of Saint Cyprian* when you have it in your hands?"

"I don't know." Heath shook his head, the questions making him feel as though he didn't have his life together at all. "Destroy it, if I can? I don't want to use it, and I *know* I don't want it to go to someone like my uncle, or Vizinha."

"Finally, if you inherit your uncle's power, what will you do with it?"

"My uncle's the kind of man who'd boil a live black cat for the bones, and I'm not. I don't think inheriting his power is really a possibility—"

"Assume it is."

"I ... I think he has a lot of bound spirits. Most of them I'd want to set free." Heath shuddered. "But I get the feeling that not everything my uncle has bound is an innocent victim, and I just don't know what I'd do with the bad ones, apart from trying to keep them from harming anyone."

Heath shrugged helplessly.

"I just don't know what more I can say than that."

"You've said enough. Thank you, Heath Cyr. I taste no falsehoods in your speech."

"Then this conversation is over," said Heath, standing up. "You are to hear nothing more until I address you directly with the phrase, 'hey, ghostie.'"

No response, which was as it should be.

"Free it," said Colin.

Nariko gave Colin a raised eyebrow and put her fists on her hips, but before she could speak, Heath asked, "Why?"

"Just a feeling. I think you'll be glad you did."

Heath ran his lips around while he pondered that. He pulled the cork, and the spirit rushed out of the bottle, through the ceiling, and off to return to its master.

As Heath watched it go, he hoped he wasn't making a terrible mistake.

Heath stared at the eggshell white paint on the ceiling of Colin's photo-ready kitchen. Specifically, he stared at the spot where his uncle's little ghostie had departed the grounds.

"Brilliant," said Nariko, fists still on her hips and anger in her eyes. "Bad enough we're flailing around for resources – and we still haven't gotten to *start* looking for this stupid book – but you have to keep giving away what little we do gain."

Heath slumped back down onto his kitchen stool. The hazelnut promise of the coffee in his cup didn't seem so encouraging as it had a moment ago.

"Tone it down a little," said Colin, softly. "He—"

"No," said Nariko. She slapped one hand down on the cold marble. "Heath, you need—"

"I *need* you to stop yelling at me," he said, his chin rising into a firm jut. "If that had been your intuition saying to let the ghostie go, and you got to make the call, would you have done it?"

"Yes," she said, without losing an ounce of challenge in her tone.

"So would I. Because doing what we do means trusting our own intuition. And I trust you two, which means I have to trust you to monitor your own flares of intuition against wishful thinking. You wouldn't tell me to turn right when every instinct screamed to turn left. Colin's told him letting that ghostie go would be better for us than holding onto it. Didn't it, Colin?"

"Yes," said Colin, sounding like he wished he were anywhere else, "though I can't explain—"

"That's why it's intuition," finished Heath, eyes still meeting Nariko's. "Now I've been dealing with a lot of assaults from the outside, and I've given both of you ample opportunity to tell me to go to hell and let me deal with this bullshit on my own. Haven't I?"

Nariko's eyes narrowed slightly in the manner that meant *get to the point*.

"No," said Heath. "You answer the question. Haven't I given you ample opportunity?"

"You have," she said, though her tone conceded nothing.

"But you both say you're willing to stand with me, and I appreciate that more than I can say. But it's still my neck on the chopping block. That means I still get the final call about how things get done. That's how it has to be, and you know it."

A single nod from her, which was as much concession as he expected. They did, after all, break up for a reason.

More than one, really.

"Good. So no more bullshit. No more lectures. I don't mind being questioned, but I can't fight the forces out there if I'm constantly fighting in here."

"I think you made a mistake letting that spirit go."

"I get that. But it's done now, so we'll just have to wait and see." Heath drew a deep breath. "So will you ease the fuck back?"

Suddenly Nariko started blinking. Rapidly. She pulled back. "I'm sorry. I just..."

Heath had the sudden sinking feeling that he'd said exactly those words before in exactly the same tone.

Nariko started to turn away, but Heath hopped off the stool and grabbed her by the shoulders.

"I need you for this, Nari," he said softly. "I don't want that to be true any more than you do. But there it is. You're smart, cautious, and you know me better than anyone. Besides, I'm seriously outgunned, and you're a heavy hitter. But if I have to second-guess everything I do, I'll be a corpse before this day is over. Or worse."

"He's definitely too pretty to be a zombie," said Colin.

That got a chuckle out of her, though Heath just shook his head.

"Everyone talks about my looks," he said, "but I do have a brain, you know."

"Yes," said Nariko, "but you're—"

Colin finished with her. "—dumb in all the wrong ways."

"Wow. I get more respect from my landlord than from my friends. That's a sad state of affairs."

"True," said Colin, "but on the other hand, if Nariko used *two* spikes she could keep her hair up even when she needs a weapon."

"She'd just draw both of them anyway."

"*All right, Brainiac*," said Nariko. "What's the plan?"

"Well, assuming a freaking meteor strike doesn't interrupt us this time" – Heath looked up, ducking his head slightly because the last couple of days had been just that bad, but all he heard was the rain on Colin's back porch – "I think we need to see about getting our hands on that book before someone else does."

"Excellent," said Colin. "I think a locator spell would—"

"Nope," said Heath, smiling as he pulled the bookmark out of his wallet. "We aren't going to chase it. We're going to call it to us."

"Um," said Colin, "not that I mind using this place as our base of operations, and goodness knows the two of you improve the décor, but I'm pretty sure my homeowner's insurance doesn't cover mayhem."

"Don't worry then," said Heath, with a smile. "We won't be calling it here. No, I think for this we need to go to one of those places of power the little ghostie mentioned."

"Heath, it's pouring down rain," said Nariko, more disbelief in her voice than suspicion. She probably already knew where he had in mind.

"Yes, it is."

"You mean that nice, dry spot under the I5 bridge, right?" asked Colin. "The one that troll haunts all winter?"

"That'd be fine for you and me, but for Nariko..."

"Wait, really?" Nariko practically bounced. She looked even happier at the prospect than she'd been to watch Heath work with poppets. "I think I still have your old hiking boots at my place..."

"You don't mean..." Colin let his words trail off.

"Yep," said Heath. "We're heading for the Witch's Castle."

10

———————

So far as Heath knew, no actual witches had ever lived in what the locals called the Witch's Castle. Rumors said it was the site of the first hanging in the state of Oregon, which had something to do with star-crossed lovers or some such. Officially it was built in the 1950s to be a bathroom, though it was mighty big for that purpose, and Heath had never seen any signs of plumbing. Either way it was abandoned decades ago.

Since then all sorts of haunted activity was attributed to it, from ghostly visages to "plasma orbs." Whatever those were. Of course, an abandoned stone ruin in the heavily hiked and biked Forest Park was pretty much guaranteed to get rumors of hauntings.

In this case, however, those rumors happened to have some basis.

Forest Park itself was aptly named. Acres and acres of trees and trails in the hills of Portland. Even a determined hiker would need days to see it all. Miles of Douglas firs and hemlocks, cedars and maples, black cottonwood and even western yew. And in between all those trees a vast swath of ferns and bracken, and more thimbleberry, salmonberry, and blackberry than anyone could want.

The place dripped with life on its driest day, and Heath knew every trail well. He harvested many herbs near the trails of this park, no few of which grew because he had planted them.

In the pouring rain like today the wet and green looked as though Heath were hiking into the essence of life itself. Heath's ears worked with his eyes toward this image, with creaks and rustles everywhere as the wildlife scurried about its business and the rain splished and splashed the creeks and rivers that ran through the park as though replenishing the lifeblood of the earth.

But Heath's nose was the first to warn him of the lie, and its warning came on the biting teeth of a cold wind. Heavy, the smell of mud and decay. Not the simple, clean smell of wet dirt he enjoyed from his porch, but the thick aroma of the full cycle of life, from the dead trees and plants, and from the dirt of the trail that had been overwhelmed to a muddy mess.

A muddy mess that forced Heath to use Colin's spare set of trekking poles. The three of them must have looked quite a sight. Translucent white rain ponchos over their clothes, calf-high hiking boots. Two of them struggling with their poles and footing for every yard they gained up the hill, while Nariko practically danced along the way.

Heath had known that her Shugendō practice had meant lots of climbing and some kind of bond with hills and mountains. But until he had to follow her up the trail in the driving rain, he had no appreciation for her ability to make mountain goats look klutzy.

Heath had no idea just how long took him to churn mud into the right amount of distance covered, but by the time Nariko called back, "We're there," he had long since regretted coming here. Yes, this was one of the best possible locations for Nariko's magic without leaving Portland – and probably the only one he and Colin could have reached in current conditions – but there was no way giving her that magical leg up was worth wearing both himself and Colin to the bone.

But finally Heath was able to stop and look once more on the Witch's Castle.

It might once had had a peaked roof, but the roof was gone now.

Only the stone remained. Two stories of fitted stone with two stone stairways leading up, one at each end. Arches where doors might have been, and three windows on each of the two peaked walls. The city had added a guard rail to keep anyone from falling back down to the trail, but the second floor wasn't where the action was.

The first floor had two rooms. One big and rectangular, little more than three walls and a stone floor. The other small and square, with an arched doorway. The smaller room was beloved of druggies. It smelled like pot year round, and today was no exception. And both rooms served as canvases for the spray-can aficionados. Both had layer after layer of tags and names and pentacles and more in a chaos of reds, silvers, whites, and blacks all over the walls and ceilings.

The floors were oddly untouched.

Heath and Colin collapsed on the untouched floor of the larger room – Heath trying unsuccessfully to convince himself that he didn't smell old urine – while Nariko ... climbed, or perched, or got ready to yodel for all Heath knew.

All he really cared about at that moment was getting air into his sweaty, exhausted body. Even the stone floor felt comfortable enough to sleep on just then.

"Heath..." said Colin, "why the fuck ... are we here?"

"You and me ... don't have ties ... to land...."

"Exactly." Colin rolled over onto his side, his face flushed so bad it looked like a severe sunburn. He panted before he managed, "So why..."

"Hills and mountains ... Nariko ... serious power bump..."

"Fucking ... better be..."

"Honestly," said Nariko, stepped just inside and out of the rain. "Just because neither of you hikes as often as you should—"

"Fuck ... you," said Colin.

Heath started to chuckle, which was difficult without breath. But it helped lighten the moment. Colin tried to snicker, seeming to let go some of his own angry frustration at the effort of getting here. Nariko just smiled and waited for the two of them to catch their breaths.

Several minutes later, Heath was sitting up, sipping water from a bottle Nariko carried in her hiking bag, and munching on a handful of cashews and brazil nuts. Colin hadn't sat up yet, but he had his own bottle of water waiting for his attention, and the bag of mixed nuts lay between them.

"There is another reason," Heath said, "for coming out here."

"Better be," said Colin, though without as much venom as earlier.

"How much advantage do we now have over anyone who tries to come interfere?"

"Exactly," said Nariko. "They'd have to good hikers or bikers – or just generally awesome like me – to get here and still have enough energy for a fight."

"Dirt bikes," said Colin.

"Noisiest things around," said Heath. "And banned in the park. You better believe the neighbors would get the cops – or maybe it's the rangers – out here to put a stop to it before they ruined the trails."

"Hope you're right," said Colin, cracking open his water bottle and taking a long swig.

Heath hoped so too.

TEN MINUTES LATER, HEATH HAD STRIPPED OFF HIS RAIN PONCHO AND stashed it in the corner of the bigger stone room alongside Nariko's and Colin's. The corner that smelled least like old urine. Now he knelt in that corner and unzipped his backpack, his head deep in thoughts of herbs and incenses and ways he might draw on the connection between the bookmark and the book to bring the latter to him.

"Let me do it, Heath," said Colin. He stood beside Nariko just inside the missing wall that formed the only entrance into this room in the old ruined stone building. Lightning flashed behind him, showing Heath what his ears had kept assuring him – the rain continued to come down heavy. "You're too close to the bookmark already. If you use it for magic—"

"I risk tightening the bond. I know." Heath shrugged. "But let's face it, that's the very reason it's much more likely to *work* if I do it. And we may not get two shots at this. Our first attempt will alert at least some of our contenders – definitely my uncle – that we have the bookmark. We need this to work the first time or all the attacks that have been failing to reach us will start coming on strong."

Heath expected some comment from Nariko, but she looked only half there. Probably on the outskirts of a Shugendō meditation he'd seen before. Something she used to contact the spirit of a hill or mountain. Most of her attention was either inward or down.

"I'm still not convinced that failure is our worst option," said Colin, moving back and forth restlessly, despite clear fatigue. "And before you remind me what the Sybil said, just remember her prophecies don't exactly come with a money-back guarantee. And the Greek tragedies are full of people trying to gain advantage through prophecy. Ask me how well it works out for them."

"I've read the classics," said Heath, now digging around, but his hand not settling yet on so much as a candle. Were Colin's words that distracting?

"Then you know they end badly. Every one."

"Colin," said Heath. He waited until Colin stopped fidgeting and looked at him. "I'm doing this. And I'm doing this now. You can either help me or meet me at the car."

"I'm trying to help," he said softly. "But you're not letting me."

Heath shook his head. "The book seems to be picky about who it goes to. Right now I've got the bookmark, which means I've got the edge. But if I let someone else do my magic for me? It sends the wrong message. Might undo everything we've been struggling for."

Colin looked away.

"Colin," said Heath slowly, "you don't want the book. Do you?"

"No," Colin said too quickly. Then he looked over at Heath, chagrin on his face, but a light in his eye. "Not really. Not to use. But" – he put his whole body into a shrug that never reached his eyes – "I love grimoires. I'd love to add it to my collection, read it through once or twice..."

Heath closed the distance between them in three quick steps and slapped Colin hard across the face, a sound that rang out from the close stones behind him.

"Wake the fuck up," said Heath. "Do your relaxation exercises or summon your Swami Force or whatever the hell it is that you do, but you get control of yourself right now."

Colin rubbed his cheek, his eyes damp with tears that told Heath his blow might have been a little harder than necessary. But Heath wasn't sorry. Better to err on the side of caution than lose his friend.

"You know as well as I do," Heath said, "that this is no ordinary grimoire. It's the goddamn unholy relic that once belonged to a goddamn saint. This is not something you can tuck away on a book-shelf and forget about, and if you doubt me ask yourself just how close you came to calling it *the precious.*"

Colin blinked and looked down. He mumbled something, and though Heath couldn't make out the words, he had no trouble inter-preting the apology they contained.

"I'm sorry too. I'm sorry I had to hit you. If you think I was wrong to do it, I'll give you a free shot to my chin. Right now, or when all this is over."

Colin shook his head.

"All right then. You need to get ready anyway, because if this works we're going to get hit like the beach at Normandy. Right?"

Colin nodded, and gave Heath a weak smile as he turned away.

But something still bothered Heath about the way Colin moved. Too slow. More exhausted than even that trek should have made him.

"Colin," he said, "want me to cleanse you with incense? Just in case that book or bookmark has a hold of you?"

"It does," said Colin, "and I'll get it. You need to focus on what you're doing. The Amazing All-Cleaner will fix me right up. And if it doesn't, I give Nariko permission to knock some sense into me."

Nariko didn't turn at that, but Sheath saw the set of her jaw change in her profile. Amusement?

"You know she's trained to hit people," said Heath. "I mean, I *can* hit harder. But she *will* hit harder, you know?"

"I know," said Colin.

And Heath realized that Colin meant it. His own little way of making sure he followed through on that cleansing rite. Fear of a good, solid punch.

Heath tried to hide his smirk at that as he turned back to his bag of tricks. *Only a man who's never really been hit can be that afraid of a punch.*

And Heath had been hit more times than he liked to think about. Fortunately, he tended to give as good as he got.

And as he looked at the contents of his bag and considered what he was about to do, Heath decided this had to be one of those times when he hit back just a little harder.

To Heath, the real trick of hoodoo wasn't learning what herbs were useful for what purposes, or how to blend the oils, or even how to talk to those herbs and roots so their little spirits would wake up and do the things he needed done.

All of that came naturally, and Heath expected that the same could be said of anyone who took more than a step or two down the path of conjure.

No, to Heath the real trick wasn't understanding how to put together solutions. It was figuring out the problems themselves. Once Heath understood a problem, the solution looked pretty darned obvious. Need to break up a couple? Black Cat Oil would handle it in short order (and it only needed the hairs from the cat, and the cat could be alive and well and purring the whole time, thank you very much, Uncle Andre).

Short of money? A little arrow root, used right, will bring in a quick gambling win that can keep creditors away and supply much-needed breathing room.

But the case of the *Black Book of Saint Cyprian* just wasn't as simple as all of that. Heath knew plenty of charms and workings to bring things to him, but most of those worked for a *class* of things. Any single copy of this mass-produced compact disc. Any old red

Corvette that had just the right accessories in just the right condition.

Specific, yes, but not exact. A Corvette *like* this one, not *this very one.*

That wasn't the case here. The book Heath had to call up was exactly one-of-a-kind, and it had at least some of its own magic to boot. Heck, if the Sybil was to be believed, the book itself might just be sentient and capable of making its own decisions.

In that sense, Bend Over Oil might have been the way to go. Just reach out and compel that old grimoire to find its way to Heath under its own power. Control its will like controlling a boss who's been refusing a raise to a deserving employee.

But that didn't feel quite right either. And what was more, Heath was more than certain that every two-bit caster with an ounce of magic in his pocket had to be flinging just about every spell he knew to try to grab this tome.

At least, it certainly felt that way to Heath.

So maybe a working wasn't the answer here.

Heath sat there in the middle of the cold stone floor of that room in the Witch's Castle. Rain continued to come down like it was November and not July. The afternoon sky looked dark as evening even though the sun wasn't due to set for hours.

Nariko stood at the missing-wall entrance, her mind deep in conversation with the spirit of this hill, which was one of the bigger and older hill spirits in all of Forest Park. Colin stood just a few feet from her, his head deep in his own magic, which appeared to have cut him off from whatever urge had him starting to lust after the *Black Book.*

For now, anyway. Once the book was here, who knew?

Heath flared his nostrils in a long, deep inhalation of the sage incense smoking up from the bedpan. Using it to cleanse the room before getting started had been a good idea, but honestly Heath cared more about giving himself a break from the smells of pot, old urine, and wet foliage.

There was old magic here. Heath could feel it in the strong, stone bones of this house. Maybe it had only been built as an outhouse – if the official story was to be believed – but Heath knew that the site had been used for magic many times. Maybe because of the power in the Douglas fir just behind the ruin, the biggest and oldest in Forest Park. Maybe because of the "ley lines" or whatever the people who studied the flow of power liked to call it.

Back down in Louisiana, they would talk about the *pwen* of this place. A point of power. Thick as a bayou swamp, and maybe just as tricky. Heath could feel it in his bones, and it sang to him to use it. To call it up and do something with it.

Power hates to be ignored.

And by the time Heath was ready to leave this place, he knew he would touch that power more than once.

What he wasn't sure of was whether or not he needed it to call the book.

All normal approaches and techniques said he did. Take the power, shape it the right way, and send it out to do his bidding. The essence of most magic, whatever form or system and whatever they call those steps.

But something in Heath was tickling at him, saying, "not this time." Three times now he'd started to dig through his backpack for his usual tools. And three times he'd pulled his empty hand back out because nothing felt right.

Some people wanted to make magic a science. Figure out how to make it something anyone can use by following exactly the same steps every time to get exactly the same result. But in Heath's experience, that just wasn't how it worked. At least, not the kind of magic *he* did.

Conjure was an art form.

And right now, the artist wanted to paint without his palette.

Heath dropped the lid on the bedpan and stood up. He stretched his sore, tired muscles and listened to his joints popping and cracking as though the hike up here had aged him thirty years.

But when he stood tall at last, he drew a deep breath and rushed it out like it was late for a movie.

He dug the bookmark out of his wallet. Royal red with soft gold fringe, and a heptagram of the same gold woven into the middle of the soft fabric. No more than two inches wide and four long, it could almost look innocent. He put the black leather wallet back, but the bookmark he held up before him. It tingled in his fingers now, like it had just maybe a thousandth of an amp running through it.

Or maybe it was excited. Maybe it knew what was going to happen.

Heath looked at it, and in a whisper he started talking to it.

"You and me, we both know I didn't put you back in my wallet this morning. You can pretend all you want, but you made that happen."

Heath waited a moment, listening with his whole being, just in case the bookmark had something to say. But he could hear only the rain, and the wind through the trees, and the gentle roar of distant thunder.

Well, he also heard the thump of his own heart making sure he didn't forget how nervous he felt. As though the beads of sweat on his forehead weren't enough reminder.

"Fine, you keep your own counsel. I won't take it personally. But if you have nothing to say, then I imagine you aren't going to deny it if I say you're nothing but a scout for the grimoire itself. Isn't that right?"

No response. Except maybe, just maybe, it might have felt a little warmer.

"Fine. Leave me guessing. Make this into some kind of test. But me, I've been tested in this game since before I ever started playing it. And I think I know what the answer to this test is."

Heath drew a deep breath. His gut grew tight at the thought of what he was about to say. His knees wanted to shake, and somewhere deep down the length of his spine, he felt a strong urge to throw that bookmark into the nearest creek and run for Canada.

But lives were at stake.

Plus, if Heath didn't do this, his uncle might claim the book.

Heath was not going to let that happen.

"All right," he said, still in a soft whisper that he hoped didn't carry to Colin and Nariko. And he said his next words not *to* the bookmark, but *through* it. "*Black Book of Saint Cyprian*, come to me. I, Heath Cyr, call you by your own bookmark, held in my hand. And I swear that if you come to me now I will claim you as my own."

The moment the last word was out of Heath's mouth, two things happened at the same instant.

The rain stopped.

A small book soundlessly appeared on stone floor in front of him. As wide as his hand and not much longer, but at least two inches thick, the book had a cover of tanned leather on the yellow side of brown. No title or author, but in the bottom right hand corner was a capital "C" as tall as Heath's thumb.

But Heath didn't need a title to know what he was looking at. He could feel its magic, like the thrum of a generator powerful enough to supply the whole Portland metro area.

The Black Book of Saint Cyprian.

11

———

Nariko and Colin whirled the moment the book arrived, turning their backs on their guard duty. Although anyone attempting to reach them at that little stone ruin still had to contend with a long, muddy, uphill hike through a heavily soaked Forest Park.

"What the—" started Colin.

"How did—" started Nariko.

"What and how don't matter," said Heath. Could the sun be warming the place so soon? The rain had stopped barely ten seconds past, but the rectangular room felt twice as warm to Heath as it had only a moment ago. Comfortable instead of chilly. And the sage incense smell came sharper to his nose. "What matters is it's here."

Nariko shivered and wrapped her arms around herself as she looked at the book. Colin shivered too, but he settled for rubbing his arms.

"It doesn't look like I expected," said Colin.

"Me ei—" started Heath, but Nariko said, loudly, "How matters a great deal. I didn't feel you touch the power of this place, Heath. How did you call it?"

"I used the bookmark."

"No," said Colin. "We'd have felt you cast a spell. And anytime you do something fast, you tend to do it loud, so we would have heard you too."

"*How* did you use the bookmark?" asked Nariko, tone sharp as a police interrogator.

"Guys, we don't have time for this," said Heath, scooping up the book and earning a gasp from both his friends. "Trouble is likely incoming, and we either need to fortify or get out of here."

Colin turned to get to work, but Nariko stayed focused on Heath. She leaned forward like she had the urge to rush Heath, but stayed where she stood.

"Tell me, Heath. This hill doesn't feel the same as it did before the book got here. Everything's clouded, like after a big stone gets thrown into a small pond. I can't read you right, and I can't read the book right either. I don't like that. So you tell me—"

"Fine. I told the book I'd claim it. Now I have, and—"

"*You what?*" cried Nariko and Colin in unison, Colin half-turning from his resumed guard post.

"I had to get the book. You both know it. And we didn't have time to play around with searching the greater PDX metro area. So I—"

"Jesus, Heath," said Colin, "you know better than to tie yourself to strange magic."

"Let's burn it," said Nariko. "Right now."

"That didn't work so well the last time someone tried it," said Colin.

Books don't laugh. Heath knew that. So whatever sensation made the book almost vibrate in his hand couldn't have been laughter.

Could it?

"It's trying to laugh," said Heath. He had to shake his hand to drop the book to the floor. Even then the sensation of holding it lingered like a kiss. Heath rubbed his hands briskly.

"Great," said Nariko, managing a step closer with what looked like a good deal of effort. "The thing's a fucking demon like some fantasy sword and it already has its hooks in you."

"I think it just found the thought of someone trying to burn it funny."

"Oh," said Colin, "*much* more reassuring. How do we get rid of it?"

"Important question," said Heath, who could feel *things* circling high above, "but not the most pressing issue."

"Bullshit," said Nariko, with another labored step. "I'd say that's now our top priority."

"We're about to have company."

"Give them the book then." Nariko managed another step, but now she was as soaked in sweat as Heath and Colin had gotten hiking here to the Witch's Castle through the thick mud. "If you claimed it you have the right to give it away. Let someone else contend with a book that can laugh at its own jokes."

Heath, in contrast to the sweat dripping down Nariko's face and the effort in her breathing, felt rested and ready to deal with these intruders.

"Our enemies are mobilizing. My uncle's got spirits homing in on us, and he's not the only one."

"He's right," said Colin. "My watchers are reporting three groups moving in. Spirits in the first wave, pinning us down while others get here physically."

"Let them," said Heath. "I'm sick of running, and if I have to risk my life and my soul to destroy this book, I might as well get to wield the power at least once."

"Touch that book's power and you stand alone," said Nariko.

"A little harsh," started Colin, but Nariko cut in over him.

"I mean it. Who knows what happens if you start using its magic?" She stopped almost in reach of the book, spending visible effort to slow her breathing. "You made me promise to kill you if the book corrupted you. Well I don't want to do that, so what say we skip the corruption part entirely?"

Heath had forgotten just how good Nariko looked when she was sweaty with effort. The way it made the jade of her eyes even more vibrant. They way her clothes hung tight to her curves. He wished he were close enough to smell her jasmine and rose body wash. Ridiculous that they weren't together anymore. But Heath could have her again. A simple spell. The *Black Book* would open right to it for him. Then she would fight beside him without question, and at the end of the day she would welcome him into her bed.

A pagan like her could never resist that spell. She wouldn't have a prayer...

"Gah!" yelled Heath, grabbing his head with both hands and throwing himself backwards. He stumbled to the back wall. The cement felt warm as a summer sidewalk.

"Not like that!" He yelled. "Never like that!"

"Heath?" said Nariko, fear in her voice where there should have been excitement. Passion. And there could be again. There would be again. He needed only—

"Never!" he yelled again. "Forget it, book. Keep your lust spells to yourself. I claimed you, but I never promised I'd *use* you."

A section of stone floor slammed upward, throwing Nariko and Colin out onto the muddy trail and slamming closed with the finality of a tomb. It was as though that section of flooring had been on hinges, made to seal someone inside.

Heath sat alone in the darkness with the *Black Book of Saint Cyprian.*

The book began to glow red.

The stone wall behind Heath felt hot now, forcing him to stand straight to get away from it. And he could feel the heat from the smooth stone floor, baking the mud on his hiking boots. The room even smelled hot, old urine and dog feces growing pungent as their residue cooked off. Not a taste Heath enjoyed with each rapid breath.

And in the center of it all, the only thing Heath could see in the pitch black room. The *Black Book of Saint Cyprian*, glowing red.

"Only so much air in here," Heath said, lowering his hands from their grip on his head. He could feel sweat starting up again, under his arms and down his back. And his legs were achy and tired once more from the hike. Whatever the book had done to make him feel refreshed, it must have undone. "If I suffocate I won't be much good to you."

But then, an owner who wouldn't use the book wasn't much good to it either. If Heath died in here, someone else would be free to claim it.

It hadn't really been fair to trick the book like that. Pretend to be interested just to get it away from everyone else.

"I'm not sure you have a right to talk about fair," Heath said aloud. Those previous thoughts may have been in his head, but they didn't feel right for his mind. He figured that, like the lust spell talk, they had to be coming from the grimoire.

But he was being too judgmental. The grimoire was nothing but a book of spells, assembled by a master magician and abandoned over a petty disagreement. Not all its powers were dark. In fact, there were spells inside that could help Heath. Help his friends. Help stop his uncle—

"My uncle," said Heath. "He's on his way right now. Probably first on the scene, as always."

And Heath was trapped inside the Witch's Castle, unable to help his friends. Nariko and Colin were good – better than Heath in some ways, or at least better than Heath had been before taking up the book – but they didn't know anything about the tricky mindset of a conjure man. Uncle Andre would strike from angles they couldn't possibly see. Could never prepare for. Without Heath—

"Without me Uncle Andre has no reason to fight. He's not stupid enough to risk himself with no reward waiting for the winner. As long as you're trapped in here with me, my friends are safe."

Of course, there's only so much air. Getting a little stale already, wasn't it? And the heat. All this heat couldn't be good for him.

Heath started rubbing his sweaty temples. "Papa Legba, this little fool needs your help. Hear me, Papa—"

Legba knew deals, and in claiming the *Black Book of Saint Cyprian*, Heath made a deal. No way for Legba to help him now.

"Damballah. Damballah-Wedo here me. Damballah the Pure. Dam—"

Damballah wouldn't help. Heath touched the edges of *Vodou* sometimes, but he never had his head washed by a *houngan* or *manbo*. Never taken any kind of initiation. Unlike his uncle…

"Uncle Andre converted? Then he *is* a *bokor* now."

Damballah would never hear the words of a little conjure man without a house or a lineage to point to. Heath was here, in the dark, all alone. No friends. No gods or saints. Just one little magic worker, trying to match not much more than a decade of occult experience against the spirit of a grimoire that had passed some eighteen centuries on this earth and seen sights the likes of which Heath could not imagine.

It could show Heath such sights. It could bring him powers beyond anything he had ever known. Power enough to strike down his Uncle. Vizinha. Drake. Those trench coat fools. And everyone else who ever got in his way. And even without lust magic, how much easier would his relationship with Nariko be if he started smartening up in all the right ways? No more problems with money. A home that would drive thoughts of his apartment into the unworthy past.

And there were many women in the world beyond just Nariko. Heath could—

"You keep coming back to lust. And power. But I know dozens of lust spells. I cast them for clients from time to time, but I never felt the need to cast any for myself. And as for power, I'm not my uncle."

Uncle Andre, who was the leading contender to claim the *Black Book* if Heath suffocated here. Uncle Andre, who wouldn't hesitate to use the book's magic, no matter who got hurt, or worse.

Heath ran his fingers through his hair until he could grip his scalp. He sat cross-legged on the hot floor. More heat all across his skin, the still air clinging to him.

Heath tried to clear his mind, but that was no use. The book had a direct line to his thoughts…

The book knew everything he was planning or even thinking about planning, so there was no use. He had two choices, power and the life of his dreams on one hand, death on the other.

…which meant that Heath couldn't cut himself off from the book either. No sealing it up magically, not without sealing himself up too...

But Heath was already sealed in here with it, and even if the heat didn't get him first, the air would last only so long. Then the book would drop the floor back into place and lie there waiting for a worthy seeker to find it.

The floor grew hotter still and Heath hopped back to his feet, his knees and ankles cracking and popping. The air tasted hot now, and it definitely tasted stale. He expected his flowing sweat must have been evaporating into steam, if he could see it.

Heath could end the heat. He could have fresh air. He could even walk away from the *Black Book of Saint Cyprian*, if he was positive that he really wanted to turn his back on such power. He would be a fool to do so. Not just the little fool he said he was when talking to the Lwa, but the sort of great fool who will end up as a footnote in the annals of history for what he walked away from. A bare mention in someone more important's rise to power.

But if that was what Heath really wanted – if he was absolutely sure – he could walk out of the Witch's Castle a free man. All he had to do was rescind his claim on the *Black Book*.

If Heath freed the book, it would have no reason to keep him prisoner. No reason to bake and suffocate him. If he lacked the courage to wield the book as such a great power should truly be wielded, then all he had to do was say, "Grimoire, I release you." Then the pain and suffering would end. He would have no more access to world-shaking power, but the book would free him.

"You would free me if I did that. You would just let me walk out of here with my friends."

The book had no reason to imprison an unaffiliated bystander. Only an owner who wanted it as nothing more than a trinket or, worse, to destroy it and remove its glory from the world.

Such an owner deserved death. But a great fool who turned his back on nothing less than the true *Black Book of Saint Cyprian* was not worth the effort of killing.

"Killing me doesn't release you, does it?" Heath tried to chuckle, but the heat had dried his throat until even his words came out croaked. He'd begun seeing spots in the darkness too, but he ignored those. "What happens, do I turn into some kind of guardian spirit that the next seeker must defeat to claim you?"

Dead was still dead. No more time with Nariko and Colin. No more sunshine and lazy days. No more laughter. No more fun and pleasure. No Heaven. No Hell. No place waiting for Heath's soul back across the waters. Only constant battle until his inevitable defeat at the hands of someone more competent. Like Uncle Andre.

"Fuck you, book. Kill me then."

The air ran out, and Heath collapsed.

12

———

Distant voices in the blackness, echoing and resonating into buzzing incomprehension. Each echo went on so long it took on a metallic quality. Combined they sounded less like voices and more like the resonance of someone tapping a length of pipe in the distance.

No more heat though. That was the first thing Heath was aware of noticing. After feeling damn near slow-roasted in that makeshift tomb, the cool was...

The cool was...

Heath didn't really feel cool either. Not hot or cold. Not comfortable or in pain. In fact, Heath couldn't tell if the surface he lay on was hard or soft.

Was he laying down at all? Maybe he was floating?

"You *could* open your eyes and find out. Just a suggestion."

Heath blinked, so startled to realize his eyes had been closed that he missed not recognizing the voice. Or that the words sounded tight, like they were spoken inside a soundproof room. He was too fixated on the fact that he would have sworn his eyes had been open.

"Yeah, it gets like that sometimes. Makes the whole world feel upside down. At least, for people in *your* state."

But now Heath's eyes opened, and what Heath saw wasn't any less confusing.

For starters, he wasn't in the Witch's Castle anymore. Or Forest Park. Or anywhere that Heath could recognize, for that matter. He was standing – *standing?* – in a graveyard.

But not just any graveyard, exactly. No grass grew anywhere in sight. The dirt was blacker than deep space, and just as smooth, except where the graves were. The grave mounds had crumbly tops as though they'd all just been dug, each one with a little tombstone or cross at the far end.

And there were thousands of graves, stretching as far as Heath could see in every direction but up. Up was a white-gray sky, like an enormous, featureless cloud that didn't care enough to gather its water into one place and think about raining. It must have kept all its lighting together, though, because it looked staticky. As though if Heath reached too high it would shock him.

"Best not to think too much about the sky. It might have *implications*. Wouldn't want that."

Heath started looking around for the voice. It sounded vaguely male and vaguely familiar, and more than a little amused at Heath's expense. Took a moment, but finally his eyes focused on a cadaverous man in a fine black suit and top hat, with a vivid purple vest and bow tie. He wore sunglasses with one lens missing. Bright white teeth gleamed out from his smile, surrounded by a narrow face with skin even darker than Heath's father.

The man sat on a gravestone, one shiny black boot on the dirt and the other cocked up on the stone beside him. His hands in evening gloves, not work gloves, and folded in his lap. A gravedigger's shovel leaned against the stone behind him.

As Heath stared at the grinning man, just for a moment – and a fleeting moment if that – instead of finery, the man's clothes looked decrepit. Like they'd been dug out of one of the many graves after years of disuse.

Suddenly everything made sense, and recognition of this man ... this Lwa ... in front of Heath dizzied him. He felt inside like he was falling. He held out his arms for balance, but his feet seemed steady enough on that black dirt.

Heath's voice shook when he finally spoke.

"Papa Ghede?"

His words sounded muted too, as though he didn't really have all this open space around him and something kept swallowing up the sound.

"Papa is it?" Ghede said with a chuckle. "Well, I'm not too sure about that. Better check with your mama when your daddy ain't listening."

"But ... you *are*..."

"Yes, we both know who I am, and we both know who you are. But I'm betting only one of us knows *where* you are, and I'm *positive* only one of us knows *why* you're ... where you are."

"I'm dead," said Heath. "Aren't I. That goddamn book killed me. So now what, I have to wait here in between until someone else tries to take up the—"

"You always talk this much?"

"I ... what?" Heath's guts felt steadier now, but that was no comfort. Mostly because he couldn't really feel anything. No air on his skin, no sense of weight on his feet. Not even the brush of his own clothing.

And his backpack was nowhere to be seen.

"You remind me of this local boy I know. Not a Lwa, though he'd claim to be if you asked him. Likes whiskey as much as I like rum. And he'll talk your ear off if you let him about this thing he did, or that thing, or some other damn thing."

"I don't understand." Nothing to smell either. Not even his own ... breath ... wait. Heath wasn't breathing. Not even out of habit. "Am I—"

"Loves to gamble, but he's not so good at it, which makes him the kind of friend I like to have around. You know what I mean?"

Heath patted his face, but couldn't feel his hand or cheek. But he'd definitely felt the sensation of falling. And he seemed steady on his feet...

"Am I dead?"

"Oh," said Ghede with a grin so full of humor Heath expected laughter to ring out from the gravestones. "Are you asking *me* this time? Or are you still making your declarations as though there's nothing more important in this or any other world than Heath Cyr and his problems."

"I..." For just a moment Heath had a mad urge to rant about the importance of keeping *The Black Book of Saint Cyprian* out of his uncle's hands, and the effect that grimoire could have on the world. But instead he said simply, "I'm asking."

"'Bout damn time." Ghede pulled a lit cigar out of the inside pocket of his jacket, and Heath actually could smell the high quality of the rum-soaked tobacco.

He could smell nothing else, but he smelled that tobacco.

"The answer, little fool," said Ghede, letting his smoke drift upward in the shape of a skull, "is no. And just between the two of us and these smoky skulls here" – the smoke had split off into three separate human skulls that floated, staring at Heath – "you should have known that without asking. But since it seems you need a reminder, you tell me. What's going to happen to you when you die?"

"I..." Heath shifted his lips around and realized he had a vague sense of his muscles moving. But he kept his attention on the question at hand. "I'd like to think I'll go to heaven."

The smoky skulls, five of them now, laughed, and unlike any words of this conversation their laughs echoed the way those distant voices had.

"Well, as to whether or not that's your final destination it's not for me to say. But we both know what happens to *you, Heath Cyr*, when you die. So you tell me. Because if you can't even tell me that—"

"Wait!" Heath smacked his hand against his other palm, which brought neither sound nor sensation, but the barest feeling of movement. "Papa Legba. When I die, he said he'd make sure my bones went to Mama Brigitte, and..."

"Go on." Ghede rolled the hand holding his cigar and the smoke spilling out of it formed another skull. Seven of them now.

"...and..." Heath swallowed, and he could almost feel the lump in his throat go down. "...and he said Ghede would carry my angel back across the water."

"And has that happened?"

"Not that I know of," Heath said slowly, "but you *are* here, and I'm not sure how I got where I am."

"Now *that's* a fair point." Ghede rubbed his hands together and Heath could hear the friction. "Though it does show a certain arrogance on your part to think this little part of you is your angel, but your education in religious matters is kind of lacking, wouldn't you say?"

"I..." Heath stopped himself and tried to take a deep breath. His body went through the motions, but nothing came in or went out as far as he could tell. "I'd say you're more qualified to judge that than I am."

"*Much* better," said Ghede, and the smoke from his cigar stopped forming skulls. Still, nine of them floated in the air looking back and forth at Heath and the Lwa as though watching a tennis match. "So now that we've established that there's still some life in your body, wherever that is – and I'm not going to tell you that right now so don't ask – the question becomes where are you now?"

"I'm ... between, aren't I? Not quite dead but not quite alive?"

"DING DING DING," the skulls chanted over and over. In fact, they kept chanting it until Ghede said, "Hush now."

Ghede put his lit cigar back in the inside pocket of his jacket.

"Perfect place for you in some ways," said Ghede. "Smack dab in the middle, like you've been all your life."

"I have to get back."

"Been waiting for those words. I swear, every man, woman and child who ends up here says them." Ghede leaned down and brushed his boot, the one he had next to him on the gravestone. "Most of them say it right off though..."

"Please," said Heath. "My friends need me. There's a—"

"I know all about what was happening before you got here."

"Then you know why I have to go back."

"Never doubted it." Ghede pulled a tin flask out of what looked like the same jacket pocket that held his cigar. He sipped from it, and Heath could smell the rum. "Don't know why you feel the need to go on and on about it though."

"Please, you have to send me back."

"Me?" Ghede laughed, and his skulls joined him. "Boy, I'm here to make sure you don't try to cross into the land of the dead."

"You mean…"

"If you want to go back to the living, you'll have to do that your own self."

13

Heath stumbled away from the laughter of Ghede and those smoky skulls, the only sounds he could hear. Heath couldn't walk right in this place between. The dirt, so black as the night sky, didn't feel right under Heath's muddy boots. His feet could barely tell it was there, so he lurched from gravestone to gravestone.

But the granites and marbles and cheaper stones weren't much help. It was as though Heath's nerves hid from this world behind cushioning layers of cotton. No sensations for his skin save the barest hints of pressure and muscle movement. No smells but that rum-soaked tobacco of Ghede's, though Heath's tongue reported the sweet aftertaste of Ghede's rum, which Heath had not sampled.

Above him only the white-gray nothing of the featureless sky.

There should have been dead trees to complete the image. Maybe with twisted branches and the decayed remains of old nooses. But no. Only rows and rows of graves stretching to the horizon in every direction, each looking freshly dug.

There had to be something. There had to be some hint. Some way to find out which direction he was going. Which way back to the land of the living.

Heath pushed on, his progress slow but steady from one grave-stone to the next. A name on each stone, but no hints or clues.

"This is the slave section," said Ghede, from Heath's right. The words tight and clipped, as though no air actually carried them. "If you're looking for a name you'll recognize, I'm afraid you're a *bunch* of rows away from any."

Heath turned his head slowly.

Ghede leaned against a gravestone, his top hat forward at a jaunty angle, one gloved hand on the stone supporting him and the other holding his gravedigger's shovel casually across his shoulder. His nine smoky skulls floated in the air around him, grinning their death's head grins at Heath.

Ghede smiled.

"You understand I'm going to keep an eye on you," said Ghede. "A terrible inconvenience to me, I know, so I'd appreciate your doing your part and not making me chase you though the whole of this graveyard."

"I don't want to go to the land of the dead. I want to go back."

"Maybe you do. Maybe you're lying. Or maybe you think the only way out is through, like this is some sort of epic poem."

"You mean—"

"I prefer limericks myself. *A woman once went to the Ritz / With nothing covering her tits / The men they all stared / The women all glared / But not a one noticed her zits.*"

Ghede and his skulls started laughing, but Heath only shook his head. He tried to sigh, but if his lungs drew any air, he couldn't feel or taste it.

"Here's another," said Ghede, sitting on the edge of a gravestone now. "Maybe you'll like it better."

"I don't need limericks. I need to go home."

"Well, I'm certainly not stopping you." The nine floating smoke skulls chuckled. "*A zombie is no good in bed / Especially if you want head / Their lips are sewn shut / They can only rut / And they lie there like they are dead.*"

Ghede and his skulls laughed again, and sorrow began welling up in Heath. Zombies. Uncle Andre had zombies with him, and Nariko and Colin didn't know the first thing about zombies. All they knew were the stupid movies. They...

Zombies.

Hope began creeping around the edges of that sadness.

"Zombies are between too, aren't they?" Heath said to Ghede. "They aren't living, but they aren't really dead."

Ghede shook his head. "You making another of your declarations?"

"No." Heath's hands were shaking. When had they started shaking? He ran them over his face and through his hair. "I'm asking you. Are zombies caught between too?"

"Interesting question." Ghede pulled his cigar back out of the inside pocket of his jacket. "But you're not a zombie, if that's what you're asking. Ain't nobody back there pulling your strings."

"Wait. Does that mean I'm free of the grimoire?"

Ghede chuckled. "You never hold onto one idea any longer than you have to, do you?"

He puffed his cigar, but the smoke trailed up without forming more skulls.

"Right. Zombies first. Are zombies between too?"

"You tell me. Do they get to move on to whatever's waiting for them?"

"No, they..." Heath stopped, blinking fast as he tried to make sense of things. "Wait. Part of them gets trapped, but I don't know what happens to the rest. The angel."

"DING DING DING DING DING," said the skulls, their words managing an echo that grew metallic as it faded.

"Well, if you want to get *technical*" – Ghede frowned at the word as though it tasted bad – "you have two angels. The big one and the little one. If you had a proper education, you might know what happens to the big one."

"Does that mean I'm the little one?"

"Keep asking questions like that," said Ghede leaning forward, "and you'll end up staring at the sky. *Implications* and all."

Ghede chuckled and puffed on his cigar.

"All right," said Heath, tapping the center of his forehead with the knuckle of his right middle finger, trying to keep his focus in this ... place. "What happens to the big angel doesn't matter. The *bokor*—"

"Listen to him," muttered through a grin Ghede, "throwing Kreyol around like he speaks it."

"—traps the little part, the little angel. That's what he commands. Must be what I am then. The little angel, here without my body."

Ghede tilted his head back and forth, not confirming but not denying.

"But you say I'm not a zombie. So I'm not trapped here and I'm still free."

"Never said you were free." Ghede pointed at Heath with his cigar. "Said you're not a zombie."

"You said no one's pulling my strings."

"Not the same thing." Ghede puffed again, and the smoke came out as an enormous pair of breasts that dissipated. "Free is another one of those words with *implications*."

"Well, we wouldn't want that, would we?" muttered Heath under what would have been his breath, had he any air to breathe. He leaned on the nearest gravestone, squeezing tight to get any sense of pressure at all. Louder he said, "But I'm not trapped here. Which means I can get back without someone summoning me."

"It means you *have to* go back without someone summoning you." Ghede tilted his head. "Assuming you're actually trying to go back."

"Why wouldn't I?"

Ghede shrugged, looking into the distance. The shrug of a man who knew more than he let on, but then Ghede *was* a Lwa.

"I want to go back," said Heath, stronger this time.

"So you keep insisting," said Ghede, popping one of his skulls like a balloon with the end of his cigar. The other skulls laughed. "But you're still here."

"Wait—"

"You keep saying that too." Ghede popped another skull. Seven remained. "Like I'm going anywhere."

"Can you help me with my uncle?"

"Now *there's* an interesting question," said Ghede, a slow smile stretching his dark, cadaverous face. "So you're going to fight him from here then?"

"I ... what?" Heath shook his head. "I wouldn't even know how to begin—"

"So, that's a no then." Ghede chuckled. "Thought not."

Heath let out a yell of frustration, but its tight sound only drove home how trapped he felt.

The laughing skulls made it worse.

Heath looked at Ghede, who smiled back as imperturbable as a sphinx. But he wasn't a sphinx. And Heath wasn't trying to guess a riddle and pass him.

On the other hand, Ghede wasn't trying to eat him either.

"You're not going to help me at all, are you?"

Ghede grinned and shook his head.

"Is it because..." the words trailed off and Heath leaned forward on the marble headstone. Almost no sensation at all in his body, yet Heath felt tired beyond his ability to express. "It doesn't matter. Why doesn't matter. You're acting as bouncer to a club, when all I want to do is catch the first taxi home."

"*A woman whose body was fab / Couldn't quite pay for her cab / She offered a look / The cabbie's head shook / For a ride, he wanted a grab.*"

Ghede and his skulls laughed at that while Heath pondered what he could do. He had no roots, no incense, nothing. He knew prayers, but Ghede seemed to imply they wouldn't work here. Not here in between things.

How could Heath get home?

"Is my body waiting for me?"

The question merely bubbled out as the thought occurred to Heath, but Ghede actually answered.

"Of course. It knows you weren't supposed to take off like this."

Heath swore. "I don't know anything about this astral stuff. Spirits yes, but here everything's—"

"Dead?" suggested Ghede.

"Missing. No air. No animals. No plants. Nothing. Not even *zombies astrals* waiting to be called."

"Those only come here until they're bound the first time," said Ghede, gesturing to the graves with his cigar. "Then, it appears that even they have better places to be than you do."

"This isn't dirt I'm standing on. I'm not really here either. And neither are you."

Ghede cleared his throat.

"Well, maybe you are, but you're a Lwa."

Ghede nodded.

"So I don't have to fight to get back. I don't have to *do* anything." Heath looked at Ghede for confirmation, but Ghede was swirling his cigar in the air, spinning his smoke skulls in loops. "Do I?"

"You tell me," said Ghede, not bothering to look over.

"This fragment of me should want to rejoin the body. I should try to just ... do nothing."

Heath lay down on the not-dirt. He let his eyes fall closed. He stopped trying to smell the air. Tried not to shift about to make his boots more comfortable. And most of all, tried to think about nothing.

That part wasn't working. Heath was worried. About Nariko and Colin. About his body. About his uncle. About the *Black Book*.

Normally, Heath would try deep breaths to clear his thoughts, but he couldn't even let himself do that. So he tried imagining this was a dream and he needed to wake up.

Heath had no sense of how long he lay there, trying to do nothing. He did know that when he opened his eyes, he was still in that graveyard. And Ghede was still right there, leaning against a gravestone, with his gravedigger's shovel standing up in the not-dirt in front of him.

The skulls were gone though.

"It's not working," said Heath.

"Doing nothing usually doesn't accomplish very much," said Ghede, who then took a swig of his rum.

"But nothing's holding me here." Heath sat up. "Wait. Is something holding me here?"

"Ding ding ding ding ding," said Ghede, in a mocking voice.

———

HEATH LOOKED UP AT GHEDE, HOPEFUL THAT MORE INFORMATION would be forthcoming, but Ghede appeared interested in buffing a spot out of his tin flask.

Heath buried his face in his hands. Stuck between worlds in a semblance of a graveyard, with no smells (except rum-soaked tobacco from Ghede's cigar), no wind, nothing. Only endless graves in the space-black dirt, and the cadaverous Lwa of the dead, Papa Ghede, in purple and black finery that, every so often, looked decrepit for a moment.

"Wait," said Heath, and Ghede snickered. "Why you? Why not Baron Cimitière? Isn't guarding graveyards his job?"

"Might be your best question yet," said Ghede with a broad smile. "Follow it."

"Because this isn't an actual graveyard you're guarding. It's the land of the dead. No! It's the place between, but you're *guarding* the land of the dead, keeping me out because I don't belong there."

Ghede winked.

"So you're Ghede Brav."

Ghede bowed, burping as he straightened up. He drank more of his rum.

Heath thought about that for a moment. Brav was more of a guardian, but there was a Ghede who functioned more as a psychopomp. A psychopomp usually only ferried people *to* the land of the dead, but still...

"Could Ghede Nibo bring me back to the land of the living?"

"Perhaps. But Nibo isn't here." Ghede Brav slipped his flask back into his jacket's inner pocket and pulled back out his lit cigar. "You are here. And I am here."

"All right," said Heath, trying to convince himself that his line of reasoning had somewhere to go. He had trouble feeling confident, sitting there on dirt that didn't feel like dirt, under a gray-white sky that...

"If" – Heath raised one finger and Ghede Brav mocked him by mirroring the move with a deadly serious expression – "and understand I don't want to do this. But *if* I wanted to try to get past you to the land of the dead, where would I find the entrance?"

Ghede Brav chuckled and smoke from his cigar formed another grinning skull that promptly split into three, all laughing at Heath.

But Ghede Brav did answer the question.

"All around you, little fool. All around you." He waved his cigar to gesture toward all the graves. "Each and every one an opening to the land of the dead, if you know how to pass through. Helps to be dead for that part."

"That's not all there is to it though, is it?" said Heath, realization dawning within him in the brightest, most positive sensation he'd felt since before the *Black Book* appeared in the Witch's Castle. "That dirt's no different than any of the rest of it. It's just disturbed because ... because a soul has already dug its entrance down!"

"Not quite," said Ghede Brav with a glance at his shovel, "but close. Don't go getting *ideas* though."

"And if the entrance to the land of the dead is below me, the entrance to the land of the living must be..."

"Say it already. The anticipation is splitting my skulls."

"Through the sky."

Ghede Brav gave Heath a golf clap. "Does that solve your problem? Are you leaving now?"

"No, I still..." Heath's words trailed off as he stared at the featureless gray-white sky. "Is that what the sky usually looks like here?"

"You tell me."

The skulls pulled together, their jaws flapping as though they whispered among themselves.

"No." Heath stood. "The black of the ground is pure. Perfect. Uniform. The gravestones aren't uniform, because no two people are exactly alike, and each leaves a unique marker behind as they pass through."

Ghede Brav puffed on his cigar, grin on his face like a proud father.

"The sky should be perfect too. But it's not."

"You're sure about that?" asked Ghede Brav.

"That's not a natural color for the sky. Not even an interpretation of one, like the black of the soil. That gray-white's a natural color for … for one great big cloud."

Heath whirled to look at Ghede Brav, five smoky skulls arrayed about the Lwa's head like a halo.

"That's it, isn't it?" said Heath. "That gray-white color isn't the sky. It's what bars me from returning to my body."

"DING DING DING DING DING," said the skulls.

"Told you thinking about the sky would have *implications*," said Ghede Brav with a chuckle. "Sounds to me like someone's earned himself a swig of rum."

Ghede Brav pulled his flask out of his coat and tossed it to Heath.

Heath worried that the rum might be some perfect interpretation of rum and overwhelm him, but refusing a drink from the Lwa didn't sound like a smart idea. He unscrewed the cap, raised the flask to Ghede Brav in toast, and brought the flask to his lips.

The immediate, initial taste was sweet cane rum with a hint of molasses. But that lasted only a moment.

What followed was the worst fiery pain Heath had ever experienced. As though the rum were distilled from molten steel. Or maybe plasma from the sun itself.

Heath fell to his knees. He couldn't even scream. Couldn't swallow, for fear of burning himself away from the inside. But his lips wouldn't just open and spit it out either.

"Dangerous, drinking a Ghede's rum," said Ghede Brav as though remarking on ordinary weather while Heath began rolling on the ground. "They use it to test our horses, you know. All those peppers and spices. Way too hot for a human being to stand. Like drinking fire itself."

No sweat on Heath this time. No sensation of muscles contracting. Only the fiery pain in his mouth that he didn't know what to...

Fiery pain...

Fire...

Heath rolled onto his back, flinging his eyes open wide. With every fiber of his being, Heath spat the rum at that great cloud. It came out like he was a flamethrower, straight into the sky and burning its way through the gray-white mass. Within the hole it left, Heath saw the most perfect royal blue sky he could imagine.

The moment that hole opened up, Heath felt himself floating upwards toward that perfect sky. The fire spread through the cloud, burning it away in silence and revealing more and more of that rich, deep blue color by the moment.

Down below him, Heath could hear Ghede Brav laughing with his skulls.

"Pretend all you like, little fool," said Ghede Brav. "You're one of ours, whether you want to be or not."

As Heath passed the burning cloud into the perfect sky everything around him shimmered into darkness.

14

───────

Heath awoke with the driest mouth he could ever remember. His tongue felt like a side of beef, smoked and dried and stuffed into his mouth. But not before someone rubbed the whole cow down with hot peppers.

No burn from the peppers though. More of a rough aftertaste like his tongue had a hangover. Might have explained why his head was pounding too, a steady one-two drumbeat of an ache that could have kept a whole ship of rowers in sync.

The odorous mixture of pot, old urine, and muddy rain told Heath he was lying on the Witch's Castle floor even before his eyes alighted on their first graffiti pentagram. That one was orange, had two points up, and the word "Slayer" written above it, which Heath could only assume was some kind of vampire thing.

Heath sat up, air rasping in and out of his open mouth with a strangled sound.

"Heath!" yelled Colin, who stood just off the stone floor on the mud of the trail. Colin's long blond hair was tangled and matted with sweat and effort, and he wore his thin rain jacket unzipped to let at least some air reach his Metallica tee shirt.

But Colin didn't run to Heath. He ran to his backpack, which was next to Heath's in the back corner of the room.

What had happened to Heath? He couldn't remember anything but the dark room and the glowing red grimoire. And where was Nariko? Shouldn't Nariko have been there too? And who were those men on the ground outside? Three of them, in trench coats.

Heath puzzled through those questions in his head while his mouth tried hard to get at least a little saliva flowing. Not much success there. Heath's breaths continued to rasp, and he kept making these sharp, broken sounds.

Then Colin was there, open plastic bottle of water in his hand, offering it to Heath. Heath took the bottle in his shaky right hand and spilled water on his face as he sprinkled his tongue. Just a little at a time, while his tongue sopped up the water and began to recover something like its normal size.

The rest of his mouth ached with jealousy, and Heath risked letting a sip pass his lips and swirl around inside. He didn't even have to swallow yet, but by the time he'd drained the bottle he could close his mouth and breathe through his nose. His tongue still felt thick and hung over, but it could move now.

"I was afraid we'd lost you there," said Colin.

"Thankth for the wa-er," managed Heath.

Colin handed him another bottle, and Heath drank it slowly.

"Nariko's out there somewhere," said Colin. "We had our hands full keeping the first wave of flunkies at bay. I handled the spirits while Nariko took down the people. Something like ten of the trench coat brigade. Man, that girl has moves."

Colin made himself smirk with his choice of words, and that was normal enough to make something in Heath's gut unclench. If Colin was making sex jokes, even to himself, then the world hadn't fallen to pieces while Heath was ... out of commission.

"What ... about the thp..." – Heath cleared his throat – "spirits?"

"Oh, you know," Colin waved a hand dismissively. "The usual assortment. Nothing too bad."

Heath raised an eyebrow at Colin's attempt to deflect attention from his own work, but Heath knew Colin had been fighting for their lives every bit as much as Nariko had. And without the power boost she got from this place.

"Any major players show up?"

"Just one," said Colin, slowly. "Ah, Heath, we all need showers and food. Maybe we better get you home before—"

"So my uncle has the book."

"Kind of yes, and kind of no." Colin's brow furrowed down as though he knew what he'd seen, but couldn't quite make sense of it. "I'm not sure. There was this break in the fighting and your uncle pulled up on a little two-person, off-road cart like a stripped down dune buggy."

"Driver," said Heath, who didn't like the sinking feeling in his stomach.

"White guy, maybe twenty. Nondescript, you know? Skin not too pale or too tan, brown hair short but not too short. Wore khakis and a tan polo shirt. Never looked at any of us."

"One of his zombies," said Heath with a shudder.

"Really? Why not a big guy?"

"So no one will notice him in a crowd. Or maybe my uncle was punishing him for something. That'd be traditional. But go on. What happened next?"

"Your uncle looked around, grinning wide. Got out and Nariko started toward him, murder in her eyes. I expected your uncle to laugh or something, but no. He held up his hands like he was surrendering. Didn't drop that cane though. He said, 'I didn't come to fight you. I just came for...' then he made this ah-ha sound and snapped his fist closed in the air."

Heath sighed and hung his head.

"Yeah, maybe you know what that means off the top of your head, but the rest of us? Nariko and I looked at each other, and when I looked back your uncle was back in the passenger seat, holding up the *Black Book*. But I didn't know where he could have gotten it from, because I swear, Heath, we looked everywhere for that thing."

Heath shook his head slowly, and said, "But my uncle wasn't grinning then, was he?"

"No," said Colin, like he was impressed. "He was frowning even when he held the book up. And he said, 'when that boy shows up again, tell him I'll be waiting for the rest of it.'"

"Damn it," said Heath, shifting to sit more comfortably on the stone floor. "Nothing about this goes easy, does it?"

"What—"

"I'm bound to the book right now because I claimed it. But the book knows I don't want to use it, maybe even want to destroy it if I can. It doesn't like that. So it tried to kill me, and it offered the first real contender the only thing it could."

"The bookmark," said Nariko arriving at the edge of the stone floor, silhouetted against the trees. Her hair was loose and flowing in a breeze Heath couldn't feel from here he sat, but she was sweaty and muddy from fighting.

"The bookmark," confirmed Heath. "It looked like the book to draw a claimant, but I'm betting the actual book," – Heath looked down to his right where *The Black Book of Saint Cyprian* sat in the center of the room – "is right where I left it."

"Jesus!" said Colin, jumping to his feet. "Where did that come from?"

"Probably been here the whole time," said Nariko coming in, her eyes running over and over Heath as though assuring herself that he really was here and he really was alive. "Probably hid until its *owner* said something."

Heath nodded, and tried to give Nariko a smile. But she didn't return the smile. She looked even more worried, in fact, when she said, "Heath, what happened to your silver flask?"

Suddenly Heath realized he was holding something in his left hand. He held it up and a shiver worked its way across his skin. Suddenly it all came back to him. The land of the dead. The conversations. The cloud-barrier. And the reason his mouth tasted so foul.

"This isn't my silver flask," he said. "This tin flask belongs to Ghede Brav."

The wind whispered through the trees outside, and Heath would have sworn he heard the laughter of those smoky skulls.

15

———

An hour later Heath, Nariko and Colin were freshly showered and back in their bathrobes in Colin's kitchen. The wrappers from a Meat for Your Beast drive-through lunch spread on the table in front of them like the casualties of war. Colin still slurped noisily from his fresh raspberry milkshake, and the smell of criss-cut fries blended oddly with Colin's floral potpourri.

Over food, Heath had told his friends all about the place between and what happened there. And now, for the first time in hours, Heath felt both full and relaxed. And after the rain and cold, the warm kitchen felt downright cozy. He felt that comfy-sleepy feeling creeping across him, as though he could just close his eyes and fall asleep there at the table.

The image of the *Black Book* flashed in his head, glowing red and malevolent.

So much for sleep.

"Did you kill any of the trench coat brigade?" said Heath to Nariko. "Or were they just unconscious?"

Nariko shrugged. She'd nodded off in Colin's car on the way here, and had barely managed to make it through lunch ... dinner ... whatever that meal was. The sky was dark outside, but clear, which was as much as Heath could tell about the time. Didn't help that he could see Nariko fighting a yawn.

Colin didn't fight it. He yawned wide and loud, dragging Nariko into the yawn and, a moment later, Heath.

"Can we talk about killing later?" asked Colin, his voice just this side of a whine. "I think we could all do with an hour or two of sleep before we push this thing any harder."

"Seconded," said Nariko, stretching her arms high in that silk Welsh flag bathrobe and tilting her head far to one side. Heath remembered that look from lazy Sunday mornings, and a sense memory urged him to slide his arms around her and snuggle in.

Heath shook his head to clear it. This was not the time to…

That memory was still there, tingling along his arms and making the front of his body feel incomplete without Nariko held against him.

Heath shook his head again. Colin asked something, but Heath held up a forestalling hand. What was…

The book?

Laughter in Heath's head now. Not the amused laughter of Ghede Brav and his skulls, but malevolent laughter.

"Where's the book?" said Heath.

"On the…" started Colin, but his words trailed off as he turned. "It *was* right there on the counter."

Heath reached into the pocket of his Batman robe and pulled out the grimoire.

"You guys take a nap," said Heath. "Apparently I need to spend some time with this thing."

"Gee," said Nariko sitting forward. "I think I just got my second wind. You aren't dealing with this on your own. I made you a promise, remember."

Her voice sounded sure, but Heath could see the exhaustion in her eyes. She'd been pushing as hard as Heath had.

"I'm not going to make a deal with the thing," Heath said. "Take a nap. Both of you. That way—"

"Call your landlord," said Nariko. "You were supposed to give him the book. So give him the damn book and let *him* deal with your uncle."

"You did sign that contract," said Colin, who made no effort to sound less ready to sleep than he must have felt.

"No," said Heath. "We have some time, and if the book *happens* to get destroyed—"

"We fought off flunkies from three major players for this thing," said Nariko. "No way word hasn't spread yet that you have it in your hands. If you don't tell your landlord, someone else will."

Heath imagined getting home to find out his garden dug up and everything he owned burning in a bonfire that Suit's lawyers would somehow make legal.

"Fine. But you guys get some sleep."

Nariko started to say something, but Colin put a hand on her wrist.

"Even Heath can't leave this house or bring anyone into it without waking me up. And I'm pretty sure we'll both feel it if the book does something."

Nariko finally nodded, and she and Colin retreated to find the sleep that Heath desperately wished he could claim himself. But he could feel the book in his head now. Separate its voice from his own.

It was the laughter, wasn't it? I tipped too much of myself.

Please, Heath thought. You think you're the first spirit to ever think at me from the inside? Now shut up or I'll shut you up.

To Heath's surprise, the *Black Book* had nothing to say to that, so he pulled his phone out of his other bathrobe pocket and dialed his landlord.

Took six rings before anyone answered. "Mr. Cyr. About time. I take it you have my book?"

"I have *a* book, but—"

"Mr. Cyr, don't try to negotiate with me. We have a signed contract."

"Yes, but the bookmark you gave me has been stolen. Don't you want me to get it back?" said Heath, his sluggish, overtired brain trying to think fast. Why had he called now?

In the back of his mind, Heath could hear the grimoire's laugh.

"The bookmark was stolen?" Silence on the line, and over the buzz of their moderate connection, Heath could hear voices in the background. At least one man and one woman. "Mr. Cyr, did you *claim* the book?"

"I had to. To get it in the first place. Some major movers are—"

"I see," said Suit with a sigh. "Mr. Cyr, I'm afraid you have erred, and the fault is partially mine for not explaining your task with sufficient specificity. I've spoken to so many who want the *Black Book* that I'd forgotten you would not know some of the basic information."

"There's nothing in my contract about—"

"I know. And don't worry. I'm not voiding my offer. But if you wish to claim the reward, you must give me the opportunity to take the book from you before someone else does."

"*Take* the book?" Any thoughts or hopes of sleep were gone now, chased away by a fear that tightened Heath's veins and pumped his heart faster. "You don't mean by force."

"Don't move from where you are, Mr. Cyr. I'll be there in twenty minutes."

The connection cut. Heath stared at the phone, wondering how Suit could trace a cell... GPS signal. Had to be. Suit had money, and that bought people who could track that sort of thing. And Heath knew that Suit had already sent men with guns to take the *Black Book* by physical force once before.

Heath could definitely hear the grimoire laughing now.

"Guys," called Heath aloud. "I hate to say it, but you need to get up. We've got company coming."

"But he can't just *kill* you," said Colin for the third time.

The three of them stood just inside Colin's front door again, with the blinds still drawn. The living room with its sea-foam carpeting and pale blue furniture looked more ready for a shoot from some style magazine than ready to get shot up by gangsters.

But "gangster" was now the word that came to mind when Heath though about Suit. The kind with the money to buy men who would kill for him.

"I still say he's breaking the contract," said Nariko.

"He's not," said Heath. "Nothing in the contract guarantees that I'll survive giving him the book, and I did agree to give it to him. Heck, he'll even have technically fulfilled the terms because I'll have lived in my apartment for the rest of my life."

Nariko sighed, and Heath heard the unspoken words. *Dumb in all the wrong ways.*

She's right you know.

Quiet, you, thought Heath. Aloud he said, "I'm still hoping I'll get a chance to reason with him. There has to be some way short of violence that I can pass the book to him."

In his head the *Black Book* whistled the question music from *Jeopardy.*

"Wait," said Heath. "I can quitclaim the book. Abandon…" There was something wrong with that line of reason, but Heath couldn't think of it.

"Perfect!" said Colin. "When your landlord gets here, just do that and give it to him."

"Won't work," said Nariko, who sounded just as certain as she looked tired. Both she and Heath were back in the same smelly jeans and shirts they'd been wearing, without even the benefit of a wash.

"Why not?" said Colin. Only he had a change of clothes at hand, and now he wore a gray tee shirt that read "Queensrÿche" and depicted a gold symbol with wings spread high and a blade or something stabbing downward.

"She's right," said Heath, realization clicking. "My uncle has the bookmark. If I quitclaim the book, my uncle will probably know, and be able to claim it immediately through the bookmark, the same way I did."

In his head Heath could hear a disappointed finger-snap from the grimoire.

"Cars outside," said Nariko from the window. "Black Mercedes by the look of them."

"It's only been five minutes," said Colin.

"More like eight," said Heath with a sigh. "Let's go outside. No reason to damage any of Colin's stuff if we don't have to."

Colin clapped him on the shoulder.

Heath led the way out, Nariko taking position on his right, her eyes narrowed and her lips moving in silent prayer or incantation. Colin took position on his left, muttering something that was probably a spell that Heath didn't have time to pay attention to.

The first men out of the cars wore trench coats, and Heath sighed again. "This is just getting uglier and uglier."

The next person out was an elderly gentleman, and Heath could only think of him as a gentleman. Hunched slightly with age, his wore his thinning silver hair straight back, and he fit his gray pinstripe suit as though he'd invented the look.

Power rolled off of this man in casual waves.

"The Lammergeyer," muttered Nariko before she returned to her spells. Heath could feel power rising up through the ground to move through her too, as well as filling Colin beside him.

It seemed as though only Heath wasn't trying to show off his personal power. But Heath had his ready to go, with spells on his lips, powders in his pockets, and mojo bags offering at least a first line of defense. If he needed it, which he hoped he didn't.

But one more person was getting out of the trailing car. Suit, dressed just the way Heath had last seen him: black suit and tie, crisp white shirt. Shoes and belt gleaming black. Jet black hair and ruddy skin giving him a devilish look.

"Wait," said Heath. "The Lammergeyer is working for you?"

"Why take multiple bids when I can hire multiple contractors and only pay the winner?"

Suit straightened his tie, shot his cuffs, and approached.

"Well, this looks like quite the stand-off," said Suit. He had six men in trench coats, each with a 9mm pistol drawn and pointed at the ground, in addition to his Italian wizard. "Does this mean you've decided to try to keep it after all, contract be damned?"

The word "damned" seemed to echo in Heath's head.

"Leave this thing with me and I'll destroy it," said Heath. "But you didn't say you were coming to get it. You said you were coming to take it, as though the only way I can fulfill my end of the contract is to let you kill me."

Heath gave Suit the darkest look he could.

"I don't plan on letting that happen."

"Fuck this," said Nariko. "Quitclaim it. Let this asshole fight your uncle for it."

"Andre Cyr *is* your uncle then," said Suit. "I'd wondered if that was just a rumor."

"My father's brother." Heath looked down the street where he could just see a limousine. "You can ask him yourself in a minute."

"No," said the Lammergeyer, his voice holding only an enticing trace of an actual Italian accent. "Do not let Andre Cyr get the book."

Uncle Andre's limo rolled to a stop in the middle of the street.

"That *would* violate our contract," said Suit. "And if you think that'd save you any risk, you're quite mistaken, I'm afraid."

"I may be a little fool," said Heath to Suit, "but you're a damned fool. You've got the money to go do whatever you want. Enough to pay people to even *kill* for you. And you want to start down the magic path?"

Heath shoved *The Black Book of Saint Cyprian* at Suit.

"Take the damned thing and go to Hell."

"Now," said Uncle Andre, getting out of his limo, "let's not be so hasty as all that." Uncle Andre was still wearing his own black suit from earlier, and his red tie looked just as crisp as it had under the Burnside Bridge. "I believe that's my book."

"I have a contract that says otherwise."

Suit tried to take the book, but yanked his hand back with a shout. The skin of his fingers blistered red and cracked.

Uncle Andre's slow, percolating laugh rolled out of him as he wandered up, excusing himself past the trench coat brigade to join the standoff.

"My, my," he said. "Haven't seen so many pistols in one place since I lived in Louisiana. What idiot brought guns to this conversation?"

Heath pointed at Suit, who shook his hand around as though he could whip the pain out of it.

"Of course," said Uncle Andre, nodding first to Heath, Nariko and Colin, then turning to the Lammergeyer. "Whatever he's paying you, it ain't enough. You know that, right?"

"Are you so certain?" Power gathered about the Lammergeyer. "Nothing I sense from you or your nephew is enough to give me pause."

"But you gotta ask yourself," said Uncle Andre, gesturing with his cane. "Are you facing just one of us? After all, the boy and I may have our problems, but we're kin and we're from the Deep South. Think a man like you ought to know a thing or two about what happens when an outsider steps into the middle of a family squabble."

Those finely honed silver eyebrows drew down, and the Lammergeyer's mouth firmed into a line.

"It seems that the elder Mr. Cyr has forgotten about the men with pistols," said Suit. "I doubt any one of you is fast enough to fire off a spell before..."

The first of the trench coat brigade fell unconscious to the ground. The other five followed like dominoes a moment later.

Suit's eyes widened almost as much as his jaw. "But..."

The Lammergeyer shook his head and turned away.

"Get back here!" Suit yelled, but the Lammergeyer only waved acknowledgment and continued toward the cars.

"Don't worry," said Uncle Andre, patting Suit on the shoulder. "I'll send a consolation prize to your window one night."

"*We had a deal!*" Suit yelled at Heath.

"I gave you the book," said Heath. "Handed it to you in front of witnesses. I'll do it again, if you like. Not my fault if you can't take it."

"This isn't over," said Suit, but before he could turn away Heath grabbed him by the shoulder and gave Suit his best angry-professional tone.

"You didn't warn me about claiming the book. It's on you if that means you can't have it. I made a sincere, good-faith effort to fulfill our agreement, and I damn near got killed in the process."

"Twice," said Colin.

"Three times," corrected Nariko.

"Whatever," said Heath. "Now you uphold your end or I'll make you regret it in ways you can't yet imagine."

"I'll help," said Nariko.

"Me too," said Colin.

"Can't say I like the idea of someone reneging on a fulfilled contract with my nephew," said Uncle Andre. "Might have to take care of you my own self."

"Fine," spat Suit. "It's a shit property anyway."

And with that he clutched his hand and ran for the car.

Uncle Andre chuckled as Suit and the Lammergeyer rode away together, Suit yelling and the Lammergeyer looking away down the road.

"Nice bit of work taking down the gunmen," said Uncle Andre to Heath. "Spirits of yours?"

"Mine," said Colin, raising his hand. "I don't like people waving guns on my property."

Uncle Andre nodded acknowledgment before turning back to Heath.

"Now, boy, let's settle this little matter and get on to more serious opportunities. Hand over the book or you'll leave me no choice but to take it from you. And believe it or not I don't want to have to do that."

Heath looked at his uncle, then made a show of looking around at the neighboring houses.

"Let's take this inside."

Uncle Andre claimed one of Colin's pale blue recliners, easing into it with a sigh that sounded almost indecent. Heath claimed the other, too tense to even try to relax. Nariko and Colin sat at opposite corners of the matching couch.

Once they were all seated, the scene might almost have looked domestic. Except that every one of them sat up and forward, at the very edge of their seats, save for Uncle Andre who settled back as though he intended to take a nap. Heath could see the lie in the pose though. Uncle Andre didn't recline the chair in the least, and he held his cane less like an affectation and more like a weapon. His hand gripped just low enough to let him strike with the silver handle or the tip, as needed.

Heath wondered what little charms his uncle had woven into the cane, because he doubted the confrontation would get physical. Not the time to open up his spirit eyes and take a good look though. The amount of magic already moving about the room might prove too distracting at a key moment, if he could see it with that level of clarity.

Uncle Andre looked about, and Heath wondered if his uncle had mastered the trick of keeping his spirit eyes open without letting an excess of magic distract him. Given the way his eyes flicked to undecorated corners where Colin likely had home-brewed spirits or important junctions in his protection spells, that seemed likely.

But Uncle Andre's own spirits had to have waited outside. Heath couldn't feel them. Couldn't see them even out of the edges of his normal vision the way he usually could around his uncle.

"You've done a fine job decorating the place," said Uncle Andre to Nariko. "Especially like the touch of verbena in the potpourri. Stylish."

Heath saw Nariko fight down a smile as Colin cleared his throat and said in a patient voice, "I decorated my own home. And thank you."

"Oh," said Uncle Andre, and Heath heard his uncle's prejudices all fill that single syllable. But before Heath could speak his uncle turned to him. "And both you *and* she spent the night here last night? Must have been some party."

"Uncle," said Heath, voice tight. "While I appreciate, and I'm pretty sure my parents agree here, that you don't want to just let some stranger murder me, let's you and I not pretend we're some kind of perfect sitcom family. You don't get to judge my choices or my friends."

Uncle Andre frowned and tapped the silver head of his cane against his chin.

"And here I thought you wanted to mend some fences, boy. Maybe let bygones be bygones and try to work things out."

"I like the idea of it, uncle. But I'd trust it more if you'd stop threatening me and judging my friends."

"Well, if we're not going to discuss pleasantries – and it seems that our host doesn't have the good manners to offer refreshments – perhaps we should get down to business."

Colin started to say something angry, but Heath stalled him with a raised hand that made his uncle grin.

"All right, uncle." Heath held up *The Black Book of Saint Cyprian* and watched his uncle's greedy eyes try to swallow it up from across the room. "First thing's first. *Bookmark!*"

Heath said the word with all the force he could muster, his whole focus on demanding that it return. He had no idea if that would work, but the moment he said it, the bookmark appeared in the grimoire, marking some spell just short of the middle of the book.

"Well, now—" started Uncle Andre, but Heath interrupted.

"No." Heath thumped the book against his open palm. "You have no claim to the bookmark because you didn't find it at large, you didn't take it by force, and it wasn't given to you. The grimoire let you watch over it while I was ... indisposed ... and as current holder of the grimoire it's mine to recall."

"Clearly you don't want this book." Uncle Andre must have used just this tone to sell his farm eggs to the local stores. "And just as clearly the *Black Book* wants to come to me. So why fight this? Why not let me just take it off your hands. I'll even offer compensation, if it'll help the process along."

Indeed. Why fight this? Your uncle seems the best candidate to me, and since I can tell you want to destroy me I'll fight you from the inside while he fights you from the outside. Think you can win a two-front war?

"Heath?" said Nariko, voice tight with concern.

"I'm all right." Heath shook his head. His words were a lie. He felt off-balance inside. The *Black Book* pushed at his thoughts. Not too much, just a little to try to get Heath to either claim the book or lose to Uncle Andre.

"Must say you're lookin' pale, boy." Uncle Andre leaned forward in his chair. "More than usual, I mean."

"Water?" said Colin.

"Yes," said Heath, and an idea tickled the back of his mind where, he hoped, the *Black Book* wouldn't see. "Maybe some all around."

"Oh, *now* it's hospitality time." Uncle Andre laughed as Colin went to the kitchen. "Bet he doesn't even return with cookies."

Nariko kept a watchful eye on Uncle Andre, but kept glancing at Heath, who had his fingers pinched over the bridge of his nose. On the inside, Heath focused on containing the *Black Book*, both to limit its interference and to keep it away from the building idea in the back of his head.

But compartmentalized thinking was just one of the skills Heath needed as a conjure man. He couldn't count the number of times he needed to keep an eye on two or three different spirits while blending and mixing and recalling the right prayers or spells to make all the elements come together for a proper working.

"You don't look good, boy," said Uncle Andre in his most avuncular voice. "Why don't you let me take that burden off your hands..."

"Let's..." Heath made his voice sound tight. Strained beyond the moderate effort he actually needed to organize his mind the way he was. "...wait ... for the drinks."

Colin came back into the room with four tall, narrow glasses of ice water on a silver serving tray engraved with filigree that looked older than anything else in the house. He served Heath first, then Uncle Andre, who nodded thanks as he took his, then brought the tray to Nariko before taking his own and reclaiming his seat.

Uncle Andre raised his glass high.

"Europeans make it out to be bad luck to drink a toast with water." He grinned. "But let's face it, ain't nothing European about me. To renewing old ties."

Heath raised his glass with the others, but no one echoed Uncle Andre's words, which got a raised eyebrow from him as they drank. Heath took a moment to savor his water, which tasted clear and fresh and cold. He made a show of draining half the glass before setting it on a coaster shaped like the musical notation for a whole note rest on the cherry wood tripod table next to him.

Colin and Nariko each settled for a sip before setting their own glasses back down on the silver tray.

"Now," said Uncle Andre, having set down his own glass empty save for its ice cubes, "let us—"

"A moment, uncle," said Heath. He held up the grimoire. "This thing's as sentient as any of us, and it hasn't had refreshment."

Uncle Andre furrowed his brow. Nariko and Colin looked suspicious. And in his head Heath could feel the grimoire's distrust rising.

Heath pulled the tin flask from his shirt pocket and spun the lid off with a quick movement.

"No!" yelled Uncle Andre, sitting forward.

Heath dumped half the contents of Ghede Brav's special spiced rum onto the grimoire.

It screamed in his head. And what a scream. It filled the whole of Heath's mind and overflowed. His eyes clamped shut. He dropped both flask and grimoire as he clutched his temples in pain, bent forward and rocking until the scream echoed out into quiet.

When Heath sat up again, he felt woozy, but he was alone in his head.

"Nosebleed," said Nariko, and Heath grabbed a citrus-scented tissue from the carved wooden holder on the tripod table, dabbing at his nose.

"The fuck was that scream?" said Colin.

"That was *The Black Book of Saint Cyprian*," said Uncle Andre, distaste all through his voice, "trying to cope with a Ghede's rum." He turned to Heath. "Which Ghede?"

"Brav."

"*Brav's* rum for a necromancer's grimoire." Honest admiration in Uncle Andre's voice, and perhaps a bit of jealousy. "Where did you get that, boy?"

"Been a long day," said Heath. And it had. The little tricks he'd been using to keep his exhausted body and mind moving were starting to wear thin.

Uncle Andre nodded, and Heath noticed that his uncle's nose had a slight trickle of blood going too. Just how loud had that scream been? Colin and Nariko looked stable at least, if nearly as exhausted as Heath felt.

"Tell you what," said Heath. "If you can handle a shot glass of this rum, I'll give you the fucking book. But it has to be you, you. Not one of the Lwa riding you."

"You didn't blend that rum, did you," said Uncle Andre, the realization in his voice making it a statement rather than a question. "That flask actually belongs to—"

"Yeah. And I'm not sure how I'm going to get it back to him."

Uncle Andre rolled his lips around as though chewing on his thoughts, and Heath felt sick to his stomach. That was his dad's gesture, and Heath was pretty sure he'd picked it up. The thought that he shared such a thing with Uncle Andre was not pleasant.

"I'm not fool enough to drink that rum," Uncle Andre said finally. "And you better cap it, because Brav won't be pleased if you let it all spill out."

Heath reached down, capped the flask, and put it back in his shirt pocket. He patted it and smiled at his uncle, who slowly shook his head.

"Boy, you've come up in the world, I'll give you that. But if you think you can scare me into walking away, you don't know me very well at all. And that would be a damn shame."

"Had to try, didn't I?"

"Yeah, I see that." Uncle Andre looked over at Nariko and Colin. "And you've got yourself good allies. That's a good thing. You'll need them, the way you work. So let's leave them out of this. This is about you and me."

"We're not going to let you kill him," said Nariko. "Not if you expect to leave here alive. I guarantee you that."

Colin nodded, and Heath was startled to see the coldness in his friend's eyes.

But Uncle Andre laughed.

"If I wanted the boy dead, he'd be dead. And you two couldn't say much about it." Uncle Andre tapped his cane three times on the floor. Uncle Andre smiled. "But Kalfu knows, and Legba knows, I don't want to kill my nephew. Not the fine root worker he's become. That'd be a waste of talent."

The smile vanished as though it had never existed, not even as a dream.

"But, boy, I want that book. I could do things with that book that a goody-two-shoes like you could never even imagine. So there's only one solution for this that I can see."

"A contest?"

"A contest." Uncle Andre nodded and looked around the room. "And I think we can do it right here."

16

———

Uncle Andre spun his pale blue recliner to face Heath directly, and Heath spun his to match. *The Black Book of Saint Cyprian* lay on the floor between them, comatose for the time being. At least until the grimoire wore through whatever Ghede Brav's rum had done to it.

"I think spirit versus spirit would be a fine contest," said Uncle Andre, voice so casual he might have been suggesting a movie he would watch with Heath. "Your best against mine."

"Not a chance," said Heath, shaking his head. "I don't keep many, and I've never felt the need to call up anything as vicious as that six-limbed thing that watches your back."

"You mean Diamond?" Uncle Andre reached up and Heath could only just see hints of the thing as Uncle Andre stroked what was probably its head. Which meant Uncle Andre had managed to sneak at least one spirit past Colin's wards. "Yeah, this one here is a fine piece of work."

"Oils," said Heath. "We each whip up a batch of Saint Cyprian oil. First to finish an oil worth using wins."

"That's your first choice? You blend that many oils these days?" Uncle Andre's bushy, steel gray eyebrows rose, then his face wrinkled in distaste. "You earning your money selling spells, boy?"

"It's an honest trade." Heath couldn't quite keep the defensiveness out of his tone. Andre Cyr was still his uncle, after all, and some family habits ran deep.

"It's beneath you is what it is. All the ways a good root worker like you could make his money and you shuffle along, selling conjure hands and Bend Over Oil to idiots who are scared of their own shadows or don't know how to keep their women satisfied." Uncle Andre shook his head. "Disgraceful."

"You want to talk about disgraceful?" said Heath, pulled to his feet by his rising temper. "What about zombies? Don't tell me you're a *houngan* full of noble good by punishing those who prey on your congregation. You're a *bokor* without a *humfo*, trapping souls for—"

"You don't know shit about my reasons, boy." Uncle Andre's tone got darker than storm clouds. "Don't you dare sit there and tell me how I choose my zombies. I work with Baron Samedi himself. You ain't man enough yet to sit in judgment on me."

Heath glared down, anger as fierce as his own staring back from his uncle's eyes.

It was his uncle who spoke first.

"I'm your father's brother, and I've got a right to a word or two about your choices, nephew. You say 'don't judge me' I say fine. I'll try to stop. But don't you think you can judge me either. Try it again and this little talk is going to get downright unfriendly."

"Fine," said Heath, slowly reclaiming his seat.

"How about this." Uncle Andre tapped the floor with his cane. "We pour a shot glass of Brav's rum, and the first one to make the other drink it gets *The Black Book of Saint Cyprian*."

Heath blinked. "You mean using *compelling gaze*?"

"No, I mean by persuasive arguments. Come on, boy, do you know a thing or two or don't you?"

Of course Heath knew the *compelling gaze*. He didn't use it often. Maybe on the occasional meter maid or hyper-aggressive salesman, but Heath was sure he didn't get nearly as much practice at it as his uncle did. Still, he had to admit he was pretty good at the technique, and it would make for a straightforward contest with little risk to anyone else, or Colin's house.

Heath glanced over at Nariko and Colin, where they sat on the pale blue couch. Both shook their heads so hard their long hair whipped one another. The most emphatic synchronized "no" gesture Heath had ever seen.

"This isn't rum blended to test one of the Ghede's horses," said Heath, pulling out the flask. "This belongs to Ghede Brav. I got it in the place between, from Ghede Brav himself. Even in that place, the sip I had was impossible to swallow."

Uncle Andre rolled his lips around. "You think making someone swallow it might be too much to ask?"

"I think we don't have enough. Not if it comes down to us making one another sip it, but remain unable to make one another swallow it."

"Fine, first to make the other *taste* Brav's rum wins and claims *The Black Book of Saint Cyprian* free and clear."

"And to be clear," said Heath, "the first to taste Ghede Brav's rum loses and has to accept the loss and move on. No later attempts to regain it. The loser has to find something else to do."

Actual pride in Uncle Andre's smile this time. "Been making a few contracts have you? Good man. And we're agreed. But we need a better place for this."

"I agree," said Heath looking down at the sea foam carpet, already stained red in three small spots from bits of Ghede Brav's rum. "I don't want to risk us wrecking Colin's living room more than we have already."

"The kitchen," said Colin.

And not much more than a minute later, Heath faced his uncle across the center island in Colin's kitchen, each sitting on a fine wooden stool. Uncle Andre had his cane across his lap. Golden light shone down from the ceiling, giving the sunny yellow kitchen an incongruously cozy feel.

One shot glass of Ghede Brav's rum sat between them on the marble counter, right in the middle of a swirl of blue with another swirl of pink passing right by it. Ghede Brav's tin flask sat to one side of the shot glass, and *The Black Book of Saint Cyprian* mirrored it on the other side.

So far as Heath could tell, the *Black Book* remained under the spell – or maybe under the table, as it were – from the jigger of rum Heath had poured on it in the living room. Heath could still smell the rum coming from the book, the same as he could smell it in the shot glass. And just the smell was enough to itch at his nostrils, even though under the spices were hints of sweet cane sugar and molasses.

Nariko and Colin, under protest, sat at the kitchen table. Both had wanted to stand near at hand in case of trickery, but Uncle Andre had insisted that they stay far enough away to not cause distraction. He'd actually wanted them out of the room, but the kitchen table was six feet away, far enough to serve as a compromise.

"Ready?" said Uncle Andre, broad grin of confidence on his face. Such a wide grin, in fact, that Heath could probably have counted his uncle's teeth, had been so inclined.

But Heath was not so inclined. His insides felt like Jell-O in an earthquake. His shoulders were so tight he couldn't roll them, and he thought he felt a bead of sweat on his forehead. The *compelling gaze* worked best from a quiet mind, but Heath had a little trouble keeping his mind quiet with so much at stake. If his uncle gained *The Black Book of Saint Cyprian*, the harm he could do with it...

But Heath forced a tight-lipped smile of his own.

"I guess you haven't done this before." Uncle Andre chuckled. "Since I asked if you were ready, you have to say when we begin."

"I do?" said Heath, feigning confusion. "I thought..." He let his words trail off when his uncle started laughing from his belly.

"Boy," he said, still laughing, "you—"

"Go," said Heath.

He grabbed the shot glass and threw the rum in his uncle's face.

EVERY BLOOD VESSEL IN UNCLE ANDRE'S EYES WENT RED, AND HIS

already dark black skin got darker. His cane clattered to the floor. Both hands flew up to his sputtering mouth, his burning cheeks.

Heath smiled a calmer, more relaxed smile now as he set down the shot glass, got off his stool, and grabbed the quart of milk from Colin's refrigerator. He did hurry just a little bit back to his uncle to hand him the container.

Uncle Andre leaned back and dumped the milk on his face and into his open mouth, ruining his suit and maybe even his shoes.

Heath waited through his uncle's coughing and sputtering. Over at the kitchen table, Nariko and Colin leaned toward each other, whispering furtively.

Heath couldn't keep the smile from his face though. He'd finally beaten his uncle. He felt as though a great weight had been lifted from his shoulders. It wasn't enough to make up for nearly being buried alive as a human sacrifice when he was a kid, but it helped.

Finally his uncle looked up at him, fury in his milk-spattered eyes. But Uncle Andre sank his teeth into his bottom lip. He dropped the empty milk carton and grabbed the white marble countertop with both hands, gripping tight and breathing heavy through his nose.

"It still burns," he said through clenched teeth.

Nariko and Colin's chairs scraped back as they stood. Even out of the corner of his eye, Heath could tell that Nariko was ready to spring into action. She had that slight bend to her knees, and her hands were up in not quite a guard position. Colin had some laminated talisman in his hand, ready to use.

"Drinking the rum was your idea for a contest," Heath said, focusing on his uncle.

"We were supposed to use *compelling gaze*." The lips moved, but Uncle Andre's jaws remained clamped shut.

"Yes, but the rules we set—"

"I know." Uncle Andre closed his eyes and Heath could see him count. Then his nostrils flared in another deep breath and he let go of the counter. He reached down and picked up his cane.

"Watch it," said Nariko. "No sudden moves now. You—"

"Lost." This time Uncle Andre was smiling as he said it, both chagrin and humor in his bloodshot eyes. "I know. And I honor my bargains."

"I never doubted that," said Heath with complete sincerity. He may have considered his uncle the most evil man walking the Earth, but like an actual Satan, he tended to abide by the letter of an agreement. And Heath had slipped one past him.

"Gotta stop thinking of you as my nephew," said Uncle Andre with some admiration, "and start thinking of you as a proper conjure man. That was a fine trick you just played."

"You'd have done it yourself if you hadn't been so sure you'd win."

"Exactly," said Uncle Andre. "Won't underestimate you again, you understand."

"I know," said Heath, and when Uncle Andre met his eyes they shared a moment. Not quite the proper familial love they should have owed one another, but something closer to it than Heath could remember sharing with his uncle in many, many years.

Uncle Andre looked at the grimoire again and sighed.

"Tell me you aren't going to destroy it. Don't waste that kind of power."

Heath sighed as he stared at it. "I'm not sure I could."

"Go with that thought. And if you need someone to tutor you in its darker secrets..."

"I won't."

"Worth a shot." Uncle Andre saluted Heath with his cane, then nodded to Nariko and Colin. "Take care of him now, you two."

"He's smarter than you think," said Nariko, drawing wide eyes from both Colin and Heath.

"Maybe," said Uncle Andre. "Maybe."

And with that, Uncle Andre turned and left without looking back.

"Is he really gone?" said Colin.

"You think he won't try again?" said Nariko.

Heath shook his head. "He can't afford to start breaking deals. Spirits pick up on that kind of thing. If you're free to break your deals, then so are they."

Heath shuddered, and when the shudder finished exhaustion rained down on him. Pounded at his head and limbs.

"I think," he said slowly, eyes half-lidded, "I just" – he yawned – "lost the last of my ... adrenaline ... and my spelllllll..." The rest of the word was lost in another yawn. Heath's eyes closed, and he felt hands lead him to someplace soft and comfortable. And then he was fast asleep.

17

———

Once Heath decided what was to become of *The Black Book of Saint Cyprian*, it was Colin who found the place they needed.

Buried among the Douglas firs behind a cemetery in Lake Oswego was a stone house that looked to Heath as though it should have been built somewhere in 16th century Europe or something. Germany maybe. Smooth stones, fitted into place with a minimum of mortar and stacked high enough to include a second floor half the size of the main floor. A bell tower stretched up a third story.

The place was too big to hide, even among the trees behind a cemetery. Or it would have been, if it weren't for an interpretation of a *don't-notice-me* spell. That wasn't quite what it was. It was more like an *is-this-important?* spell, where onlookers could only see the place if they had business there.

And even that wasn't quite right, because it didn't quite feel like a spell. But that was only appropriate, considering the people who Colin said lived there.

Heath and his friends went to this building behind the cemetery on the second day after Heath's victory of Uncle Andre. The first day was spent largely celebrating, which honestly meant sleeping and eating delivery pizza and staring at whatever comedies Colin could find on his satellite television until they all felt decompressed and ready to face the world.

Only then, on the second day, did Colin run them each past their homes for a change of clothes before they came down here. Heath grabbed more than clothes, though. He also grabbed a pair of rosaries he'd already blessed in the name of Damballah, and used them to wrap the *Black Book* to make sure it stayed quiet and made no effort at persuading him or finding another host/owner.

That might not have been strictly necessary though. Truth was, the book seemed to be sulking. So far as Heath could tell, the grimoire knew it had gambled everything on Uncle Andre and lost, so as long as Heath wasn't trying to destroy it, it was going to sit there and shut up.

Which was fine with Heath. Because destroying it might not have worked anyway.

And so it was that the three of them came to be standing in the woods behind that cemetery, staring at this stone house under a bright, cheerful July sky on a pleasantly warm day. Colin wore torn, faded purple jeans and a Danzig tee-shirt featuring a monstrous skull and an inverted cross, which Heath considered in bad taste. Nariko wore her hair loose over a cream-colored, low-cut blouse and dark burgundy slacks. Heath wore loose blue jeans with a red-and-white striped button up shirt with short sleeves.

Heath had his backpack slung over one shoulder, and the rosary-bound *Black Book of Saint Cyprian* tucked under the other arm.

"You're sure this is the place?" he said.

"Look at it." Colin presented the building with his hand. "Could you picture anyplace more appropriate?"

"I expected crosses," muttered Nariko.

"Crucifixes," corrected Heath.

"Details," said Colin. "This is the place."

They approached a stout door made of thick, rough boards of dark wood, bound with iron bands. It had a mini-door that could swing open at head-height, and no doorknob or handle that Heath could see.

Heath raised an eyebrow at Colin, but lifted his fist and pounded three loud strikes.

Nothing seemed to happen.

In fact, nothing seemed to happen for so long that Heath raised his fist to knock again when finally the mini-door swung open, revealing a tanned, pointed man's face with a tonsured scalp.

"Yes?" the man said in a surprisingly gentle tone. "How may I assist you? I am afraid I'm not good at giving directions."

"Is this the Protective Order of Saint Benedict?"

The man blinked, and looked sharper at Heath's face, then the faces of Colin and Nariko.

"I feel the power you bring to my door," said the man, his voice still gentle but his words pointed, "and I feel evil among you as well. In the name of Michael I charge you, speak the truth of your purpose."

And when the man said those words, Heath could feel a single shaft of sunlight find him there among the trees. Golden sun all around him, making him glow. The need for honesty filled him, but Heath had dealt with many kinds of compulsions over the years. He knew full well he could have fought this one too, and maybe even beaten it.

But Heath had no reason to lie right now.

"I've come into possession of *The Black Book of Saint Cyprian*. I have fought battles I did not seek to keep it out of the hands of those who would use it for evil. I cannot keep it for it might corrupt me. I do not know how to destroy it. The Vatican sheltered it for more than a thousand years. I'd like to think you people can shelter it for a thousand more."

The man's eyes and mouth opened wider than the loving arms of his Savior. On such a pointed face – the man's nose must have reached eight inches or more forward from his ears – the sight made Heath laugh.

"Truth," the man finally hushed out, prominent Adam's apple bobbing. "I taste the truth and feel Michael's confirmation." He ripped the door open with suddenness and strength that amazed Heath. "Come in. Quickly. Please."

"Look," said Heath, "I just want—"

But the man grabbed Heath by the wrist and pulled him inside, Nariko and Colin following right behind him.

"This way," the man said, and Heath realized the man was wearing a rough brown robe with a brown rope belt that together looked as though they belonged in the same century as this building – and it wasn't this one.

But the man was strong and quick, and dragged Heath with him down a stone hall where torches in sconces lit up as they passed. Heath expected the smell of damp and must, but none of that here. Everything smelled clean and dry, with an undercurrent of baked bread and some kind of incense. He could hear the faint strains of some kind of singing or chanting, but nothing he could make out.

They passed two closed doors that looked like thinner versions of the front door – though each with a door handle and without the mini-door for looking out – before the man stopped.

This man, this monk – and Heath was sure this man was a monk – composed himself and knocked with five gentle raps.

"Enter," said a firm voice from the inside.

"Brother Theodopolis," said the monk as he opened the door, one hand still clutching Heath's wrist with impressive strength. "Brother, this man has brought us *The Black Book of Saint Cyprian!*"

The chamber was clearly an office. Though smaller than Colin's kitchen, its walls were lined with books that Heath would have sworn didn't look like they were printed on any kind of press at all. Any more than the desk Brother Theodopolis sat at could have been made by machine, with its finely stained finish and smooth design.

Brother Theodopolis sat on a small stool, an actual quill and parchment on the desk before him, complete with ink well and blotter. Brother Theodopolis looked as thin as the first monk, but broader through the shoulders and jaw, and with an almost square head, which made the tonsure an odd stylistic choice. And Brother

Theodopolis had a crooked nose, as though it had been broken several times and never quite set properly after any of them.

"Slow down, Brother Maynard," said Brother Theodopolis. "You are certain he truly has…" Brother Theodopolis' words trailed off as he looked over at what Heath had in his hands, twice wrapped in rosaries.

Brother Theodopolis cocked his head to one side. "Those rosaries were not blessed by a priest, but they do carry a blessing. Is this your work, sir?"

"Yes, they were blessed by me in the name of Damballah."

"Syncretized with our Lord and Savior Jesus Christ, I believe."

"As you say." Heath could feel the warmth of Nariko and Colin stepping up behind him.

"And that book." Brother Theodopolis set down his quill and sat still with ramrod straight posture. "At a glance it appears to be the genuine article."

"Considering the trouble it's put us to it better be."

"If you are a treasure hunter, you will be disappointed here."

Heath felt his lips quirk high to the left. "Hardly. I'm just a root worker. A conjure man. I never wanted to own this thing and I want to get rid of it."

"He wishes us to take it back into protective custody," said Brother Maynard. "He said so under the light of the Archangel Michael. He would destroy it if he could."

"I'm not sure it can be destroyed," said Brother Theodopolis. "Despite what the movies may imply, not everything can be vanquished by casting it into a volcano."

"Shoot," said Colin, snapping his fingers.

Brother Theodopolis opened a drawer and pulled out a square of tan cloth, perhaps two feet across, and the softest looking thing Heath had seen in this place. But that wasn't all. Heath could feel the power of that cloth. Protective. Sheltering.

Brother Theodopolis spread the cloth across both of his hands and reached out for the book.

"Two things," said Heath, holding up the book. "First, I want those rosaries back."

Brother Theodopolis nodded as though it had never been in question.

"Second, I want you to swear in the name of your God that you will get this book hidden away somewhere and protected so it doesn't get out again in my lifetime."

"By the oaths I have taken before my Lord to serve and protect his human race while blood flows in my veins and air passes my lips, I swear that I, Brother Theodopolis, shall take full responsibility and accountability for *The Black Book of Saint Cyprian* until it can be hidden away behind the walls of the Vatican where it shall be guarded by such angels as He will spare for the task."

"Good enough," said Heath with a nod. He placed the book on the cloth, and Brother Theodopolis folded the cloth to cover the grimoire completely. In that moment, Heath felt a snap, and realized that his connection to *The Black Book of Saint Cyprian* had finally broken.

He smiled with such a relaxed sigh that Brother Theodopolis smiled back at him.

"I have seen that look before, and if it helps, I can assure you that you are now free of it." Brother Theodopolis patted it. "I should like to have the rosaries delivered to you later, if I may, to maintain their protections as well."

Heath nodded.

"Excellent." Brother Theodopolis set the enwrapped grimoire on his desk. "Then there's another matter I'd like to discuss with you. You see, this is the first time anyone has ever brought a relic to us..."

Two hours later the three of them were riding through the twisting hills of Lake Oswego in Colin's Saturn, on their way to a celebratory meal downtown. Colin behind the wheel, Heath riding shotgun, and Nariko in the back seat.

But the sky was clear blue above them, and Heath could hear the birds singing. He never quite appreciated the songbirds of the Pacific Northwest the way he did just then. Like a choir of tiny angels praising the joy of life.

"Seriously?" said Colin. "You're going to work for the Catholics?"

"I may not go to church every Sunday, but I *was raised* Catholic. Besides, I'll work for pretty much anyone who a) isn't an asshole, and b) can pay me. But I never guaranteed I'd do any single job for them. I just agreed that I'd be willing to help out their order from time to time with their fighting-evil gig."

"For better rates than you've been charging," said Nariko from the back seat. "Please tell me you're raising your rates."

"After what I – what *we* – just pulled off? Hell yes."

"Halle-fucking-luiah."

"Heck, once Suit's check clears I'm probably taking a vacation. In fact, I owe you guys, so if it's a trip, I'll pay tickets and hotel."

"How many rooms?" said Colin. "I'm not sharing with you, Heath."

Nariko quirked an eyebrow at Heath and twitched her lips in a way that suggested *she* might share a room with Heath on this vacation.

Maybe.

Heath smiled, and missed the next three things that Colin said. In fact, he felt so good at that moment that he missed everything Colin said about vacations until they pulled up to a stop sign.

At the stop sign, a scooter pulled up alongside and knocked on Colin's window. In the blink of an eye, all three of them were back on guard, ready for an attack.

Colin rolled the window down. "Special delivery," said a young Latin boy. Heath saw South America in the boy's features but couldn't be sure which country. The boy held up a distinctive pink box, the sort that everyone in the greater Portland area recognized on sight.

Voodoo Doughnuts. Bizarre and wonderful combinations of decoration and flavor in the name of deliciousness.

Colin reached for the box, but Heath grabbed his shoulder to stop him.

"Who's it from?" he asked. "And who's it for?"

"It's for you, Mr. Cyr, and it's from Vizinha. She gave me a message. She said to tell you she heard about how you handled both the Lammergeyer and your uncle. She says, 'well done.' She hopes you'll consider this classic dozen an offering of peace between the two of you."

"I assume she knows this isn't enough to make us friends."

"She said you'd say that, and she knows."

"And did she swear the donuts, the box, all the contents, the delivery, and the deliverer are all clear and safe?"

"She swore in front of me. She said, 'In the names of *Oxalá* and *Iemanja* I swear that everything about this offering and its delivery is clean and safe and untampered with by anyone.'"

"He's telling the truth," said Nariko from the backseat.

"Come on, Heath," said Colin. "She even guaranteed that no one tampered with it after it was out of her hands."

"All right," said Heath, and he reached over to accept the box.

The delivery boy refused a tip from Colin and rode off.

"Is this the celebratory meal then?" said Nariko, eyebrow raised.

"Hell no," said Heath. "I want steak. But these will make a great dessert."

Nariko nodded approval while Colin laughed. But then Colin's laugh cut short. "Heath, what about that flask? The one you—"

"I know, I know," said Heath, with as much patience as he could muster. "But that, my friends, I'm going to deal with tomorrow."

SIGN UP FOR STEFON'S NEWSLETTER

Stefon loves to keep in touch with his readers, and loves to keep you reading. The best way for him to do both is for you to sign up for his newsletter.

Sign up at http://www.stefonmears.com/join

If you sign up for Stefon's newsletter, you get...

- Monthly updates about his publishing and travel schedules
- His latest news, in brief, and answers to reader questions
- A free short story for signing up
- List-only offers and occasional specials
- Plus a free short story every month!

ABOUT THE AUTHOR

Stefon Mears might just have a copy of *The Black Book of Saint Cyprian* on his shelf. Stefon has more than thirty books to his credit, and he never stops writing. He earned his M.F.A. in Creative Writing from N.I.L.A., and his B.A. in Religious Studies (double emphasis in Ritual and Mythology) from U.C. Berkeley. He's a lifelong gamer and fantasy fan. Stefon lives in Portland, Oregon, with his wife and three cats.

Look for Stefon online:
www.stefonmears.com
himself@stefonmears.com

www.ingramcontent.com/pod-product-compliance
Lightning Source LLC
Chambersburg PA
CBHW050531190726
48284CB00003B/1025